HIDDEN BLOOD

W. C. TUTTLE

SAGEBRUSH
Large Print Westerns

First published in Great Britain by Collins
First published in the United States by Houghton Mifflin

First Isis Edition
published 2018
by arrangement with
Golden West Literary Agency

The moral right of the author has been asserted

A catalogue record for this book is available
from the British Library.

ISBN 978–1–78541–559–3 (pb)

Published by
F. A. Thorpe (Publishing)
Anstey, Leicestershire

Set by Words & Graphics Ltd.
Anstey, Leicestershire
Printed and bound in Great Britain by
T. J. International Ltd., Padstow, Cornwall

This book is printed on acid-free paper

HIDDEN BLOOD

Cowboys Hashknife Hartley and Sleepy Stevens take the stage to the hot springs of Hawk Hole, seeking to ease Hashknife's rheumatism. But their journey is interrupted by a night holdup, which sees a strongbox stolen and a passenger shot. Hastening the wounded man to the doctor at Pinnacle, Hashknife and Sleepy find themselves the recipients of surprisingly generous hospitality from Big Medicine Hawkworth, the forbidding owner of Hawk Hole and the Tumbling H. There is bad blood between Hawkworth and the K-10 ranch thanks to cattle rustling, and a range war seems inevitable. After a K-10 cowpuncher attacks Hashknife in the night, it becomes apparent that there is more trouble seething than a simple ranch rivalry. The stolen strongbox was carrying funds for Hawkworth's interest in a mine. And why would a holdup man shoot a surrendering passenger?

SPECIAL MESSAGE TO READERS

THE ULVERSCROFT FOUNDATION
(registered UK charity number 264873)
was established in 1972 to provide funds for
research, diagnosis and treatment of eye diseases.
Examples of major projects funded by
the Ulverscroft Foundation are:-

- The Children's Eye Unit at Moorfields Eye Hospital, London
- The Ulverscroft Children's Eye Unit at Great Ormond Street Hospital for Sick Children
- Funding research into eye diseases and treatment at the Department of Ophthalmology, University of Leicester
- The Ulverscroft Vision Research Group, Institute of Child Health
- Twin operating theatres at the Western Ophthalmic Hospital, London
- The Chair of Ophthalmology at the Royal Australian College of Ophthalmologists

You can help further the work of the Foundation
by making a donation or leaving a legacy.
Every contribution is gratefully received. If you
would like to help support the Foundation or
require further information, please contact:

THE ULVERSCROFT FOUNDATION
The Green, Bradgate Road, Anstey
Leicester LE7 7FU, England
Tel: (0116) 236 4325

website: www.foundation.ulverscroft.com

CHAPTER
ONE

HASHKNIFE HAS RHEUMATISM

"If I had rheumatism like you've got, I'd sure head for the hot springs. Yuh can boil it out easier'n any other way."

The owner of Piute leaned back, braced his bony elbows on the bar, spat wisely, and squinted at the two cowboys, who were draped against the bar beside him.

"Hashknife" Hartley, a tall, thin, serious-faced cowboy, was standing on one leg, much in the attitude of a stork, except that his knee naturally bent the other way.

"Sleepy" Stevens, Hashknife's partner, was of medium height, with a grin-wrinkled face and serious eyes. There was nothing colorful nor romantic about their raiment or physical appearance. They were clad in well-worn overalls, nondescript shirts, high-heeled boots, and sombreros.

Their cartridge belts were scarred, weathered, as were their holsters, from which protruded the plain wood butts of single-action Colt sixshooters. They wore no coats. Hashknife's vest was little more than a wrinkled piece of cloth, suspended stringlike from his shoulders, affording him pocket room for his tobacco and cigarette papers.

"Which way do yuh head for hot springs, pardner?" asked Sleepy, making cabalistic marks, on the scarred bar top with the bottom of his wet glass. "I'm goin' to put this lean pardner of mine on to boil."

"Aw, I'll be all right," protested Hashknife, flexing his aching leg.

"You won't be until yuh are," flared Sleepy. "Yuh can't ride a horse thataway. I've done used up a bottle of horse liniment on yuh, and all it's done is to make yuh smell."

"Rheumatism ain't no fun." Thus the proprietor. "I sure had it ache hell out of me a few years ago."

"Didja go to a hot spring?" asked Sleepy.

"Shore did. I went up into Hawk Hole and b'iled out up there. That sulphur water smells like all the bad aigs of the world had been busted; but it knocked my rheumatism."

"Where's this here Hawk Hole?" asked Hashknife, interested.

"South of here, about thirty mile. I dunno whether yuh can use the springs now or not. Belongs to 'Big Medicine' Hawkworth, and he ain't so friendly as he might be."

"We'd take a chance on him, if Hashknife was able to ride that far," said Sleepy.

"Yuh might go by stage. She comes through here about midnight and changes horses here. On 'count of the heat they make the drive from Caliente at night. They go to Pinnacle; but in yore case they might swing

2

around by Hawkworth's place and let yuh off. If they don't, it's only two miles from Pinnacle."

"That sounds good t' me," declared Sleepy. "How does she listen to you, pardner?"

"Well, all right, Sleepy. I'd go any place to get rid of this ache that's twistin' my muscles. I ain't slept for three nights and days hand-runnin'. If this Hawkworth person tries to deny me a chance to boil the pain out of my carcass, I'll try and make him see the error of his ways."

"He prob'ly will deny yuh," said the proprietor. C'mon and let's see if supper is ready."

Piute consisted of one building, a long, low adobe structure, separated into three parts: a saloon, a dining-room and kitchen combined, and a place to sleep. Behind this long building were a shedlike stable, corrals, and a well.

Its only excuse for existence was to act as a stage station, or a night haven for those who traveled the road from Caliente to Pinnacle. Piute was always hot, except at night. To the north the road disappeared through mesquite-covered flats, while to the south, it twisted higher into the hills; rocky hills, where grew stunted pine, piñon, and juniper; down in a land where the law held little sway, where only a range of hills separated them from the land of mañana.

Hashknife managed to limp into the dining-room assisted by Sleepy, flopped into a chair, and did justice to a feed of tortillas, frijoles, and coffee.

"You ain't natives down in this here country, are yuh?" asked the proprietor.

3

"What makes yuh think that?" grinned Sleepy.

"Jist seen yuh blowin' on yore frijoles. Yuh can't cool no chili peeper by blowin' on it, pardner."

"My mistake," grinned Sleepy. "The danged things are hot."

"Need 'em inside yuh down here. Hot food is the stuff in this climate. Eskimo would explode on it. Never been over in Hawk Hole, have yuh?"

"Never heard of it," said Hashknife.

"Town of Pinnacle's over there. Ain't much of a town. Lot of mines back in the Greenhorn country and they all outfits down in Pinnacle. Old Big Medicine Hawkworth owns most of Hawk Hole. Stage line does quite a business, haulin' supplies, miners, and the kind of folks that clutter up a minin' town. Pinnacle ain't exactly in the Hole — kinda on the rim of it. Them hot springs are shore good for rheumatism, y'betcha. There's cold springs there, too. Big Medicine has been there twenty-five year, and he shore hooked on to most of the place."

"Does he run any cattle?" asked Sleepy.

"Yeah. He has the Tumblin' H iron. The Hole is a dandy place for to run cows, except that she's almost too close to the border."

"We might get a job," smiled Sleepy. "I'd punch cows while you boil out, Hashknife."

"Yeah, yuh might," agreed the proprietor. "But I'm bettin' yuh won't. Big Medicine will prob'ly tell yuh that yuh can't take a soak in his hot springs, and tell yuh to get to hell off his place. He's an old squaw-man — meaner than hell.

"Some folks say that Big Medicine is English, English from the old country. We don't see much of him. He's been out this far jist once since I've been here at Piute. I've heard folks say that he's crazy. I dunno whether he is or not. Anyway, I do know that he wants folks to leave him alone — and they mostly always do the second time."

Hashknife grimaced with pain as he shoved back from the table and tried to cross his knees.

"Does this Big Medicine person mind his own business?" he asked.

"Hm-m-m — well, I s'pose so. Down in this country yuh can hear all kinds of talk. It mostly goes into one of my ears and out the other, bein' as I ain't noways situated where I can talk a lot about my fellermen and keep my scalp where she belongs. He ain't never bothered me; so I say he's all right."

Hashknife and Sleepy did not ask for any further information. They were in a strange country, whither they had drifted; wanderers into the cattle country of the Southwest. They had found things but little different from those in Montana, Idaho, Wyoming, except for the desert stretches, style of architecture, and lack of streams.

All had been well until Hashknife had contracted rheumatism, which had crippled him so badly that he suffered keenly in riding. Sleepy had doctored him to the best of his limited ability, but the pain had grown steadily worse, and they both knew that it was a case of seeking medical assistance, at once.

The arrival of the midnight stage interrupted their three-handed game of seven-up. It required four horses to haul the heavy stage over the grades ahead, and the proprietor assisted in changing teams.

The driver was a big, gruff Norwegian, with a big beard and a heavy head of hair, which stood up on his head like the roach of a grizzly bear.

The only passenger was a young man, well dressed, black-haired, and with a thin, dark face. He was hardly past twenty years of age, but his mouth and eyes already showed lines of dissipation. He drank whiskey at the bar and climbed back into the stage while Hashknife and Sleepy were tying their horses at the boot.

"You got de rheu-maticks?" asked the driver; when he noticed that Hashknife had difficulty getting aboard.

"That's what she feels like," grunted Hashknife. "I never had it before, but they say she acts like this."

"Yah, she does. You go to Pinnacle, eh?"

"The hot springs."

"So? To de hot springs, eh? All right."

His long whip snapped in the moonlight, the four horses sprang into life, and the stage to Pinnacle went lurching and grinding up the grades, swinging wide on the narrow turns, where a driver is only allowed one mistake.

Over the top of the hill they swung back into another valley, a fairyland in the blue of the moonlight. The road was rough, badly engineered as to grades, but the driver swore in his own tongue, plied his long whip without stint or threw his weight on a protesting brake on the steep pitches.

The young man had nothing to say. He smoked innumerable cigarettes and huddled down in his seat. Hashknife suffered in silence, while Sleepy whistled unmusically between his teeth and cursed the driver.

"He's hit every rock so far," he told Hashknife. "I'll bet yuh even money that this damned equipage don't hold together to reach Pinnacle."

Sleepy turned to the young man. "Have you ever been over this road, pardner?"

The young man removed his cigarette. "No," he said.

"Think you'll ever go agin'?"

"Maybe."

Sleepy laughed and stretched out his legs. "You won't never get hung for talkin' too much."

"What do you mean?" asked the stranger coldly.

"Oh, hell!"

Sleepy shifted his seat and rolled a cigarette. Hashknife forgot his pains long enough to laugh. Thereafter all conversation ceased, except from the driver. Stretches of smooth road lulled the passengers to sleep, only to shock them back with lurching bumps that even drew profanity from the lips of the driver.

About twenty-five miles of the journey had been completed. The road wound down the side of a mountain, twisting around the heads of deep, heavily timbered draws and out onto moonlit points, where far below stretched the haze of Hawk Hole. Here the roadbed was more smooth and the passengers dozed.

Suddenly the driver swore viciously, shoved on the brake until the rear wheels almost skidded off the grade. Sleepy was flung off his seat, and he fell across Hashknife's lap, colliding with the stranger.

For several moments they were confused, dazed; and when they turned to the open windows of the stage, they looked into the muzzles of two shotguns, which were plainly defined in the moonlight.

"Stay jist like yuh are," ordered a clear voice. "We can see yuh plenty plain, gents."

The holdup men had their backs to the moon, which flung its rays into the stage, and Sleepy knew that a motion toward his holster would invite one or both of those shotguns to send a wicked shower of lead into them.

"Lift up yore hands," ordered the voice again, and all three men complied. "Now git out of there, one at a time."

Sleepy came out first and lined up against the side of the stage, while behind came the stranger. Sleepy's holster had twisted behind him. It was difficult for Hashknife to get out and the men swore at him for his slowness.

"He's got rheumatism, dang yuh!" snorted Sleepy.

"Excuse me," laughed one of the men. "Now line up."

One other man was helping himself to the strongbox, while the driver sat stolidly in his seat, arms reaching toward the sky. He yanked the strongbox out across the front wheel and let it fall into the dirt.

8

The man who had handled the box was carrying a revolver in one hand, and now he came back to those who were watching the passengers. The men were all masked. The man with the revolver looked at the passengers closely.

Suddenly, and with apparently no reason, he threw up his revolver and fired point-blank at the stranger. The action was so sudden, so uncalled for, that Hashknife and Sleepy instinctively ducked.

"Stand still, damn yuh!" roared one of the shotgun men.

The stranger went to his knees, groped blindly for a moment, and sprawled on his face.

For several moments not a sound was heard. Then the man who fired the shot shoved his gun back into his holster.

"The damn fool reached for a gun," he said slowly. "Shove the rest of 'em back into the stage."

Hashknife turned and climbed back inside, while one man picked up the strongbox and walked around the team. Sleepy got inside, menaced by those two guns, and sat down. The two men turned and started around the team, while Sleepy swore softly, swung his belt around, and jerked out his gun.

"Take it easy, pardner," cautioned Hashknife. "They never hurt us."

"They killed that poor devil," replied Sleepy angrily. "He never tried to pull a gun, Hashknife."

Sleepy stepped outside, gun in hand, but the men had disappeared. The driver was starting to get down.

"Held up, I'm a son of a gun!" he snorted, as he almost fell off the hub.

Sleepy knelt down and examined the stranger. He was breathing heavily, painfully, and was unconscious. "Well he ain't dead," declared Sleepy. "How far is it to town, driver?"

" 'Bout five-six mile. I'm never held up before, I'm a son of a gun!"

"Put him in here," ordered Hashknife.

Sleepy and the driver lifted the wounded man inside and eased him into a seat. He was as limp as a rag, so Sleepy sat beside him, holding him upright.

"Drive as fast as yuh can," ordered Hashknife. "This man needs a doctor right now."

"You bet you," agreed the driver. "I'll go like hell."

He was as good as his word. Hashknife and Sleepy were not at all faint-hearted, but that driver brought prayers to their lips before the running team reached the bottom of Hawk Hole. In fact he had caused Hashknife to forget his rheumatism.

"How are yuh standin' it, Hashknife?" asked Sleepy.

"He either scared or bumped it all out of me," replied Hashknife.

"I'll betcha. There's some things that even rheumatism won't stand for, I reckon. We ought to be close to town. That driver said five or six miles, and we fell that far."

In a few minutes they drove into the sleeping town of Pinnacle and stopped in front of a stage station. Daylight was flooding the hill now. A sleepy-eyed individual opened the door of the stage office and came out to them. Across the street glowed the dim light of an oil lamp over a poker game.

Somewhere a cheap phonograph screeched a tune, following a squeaky announcement that it was being sung by So-and-So, for the So-and-So "Phonograph Cuc-cuc-company of New Yar-r-r-k and Par-Par-Paris."

It did not take the excited driver long to blurt out the fact that he had been held up, robbed of the strongbox, and that he had a dying man inside the stage. The sleepy-eyed one snapped into life. He turned around twice, evidently undecided just what to do — and did nothing.

"Yore best bet is to take this feller to a doctor," declared Hashknife.

"That's right," agreed the sleepy-eyed one. "Doc Henry lives jist outside town, Pete. He ain't such a damn good doctor, I don't suppose, but he's all we've got. Say, the sheriff is here, I think. Anyway, he was here last night, and mebbe he's over there in that poker game right now. Lemme look."

He ran across the street into a saloon, and was back in a minute, followed by a short, heavy man, who questioned the driver regarding the affair.

"Is the man still alive?" he asked.

"He won't be, if yuh don't quit yappin' and get him to a doctor," declared Sleepy.

The sheriff came closer and peered into the stage. He was a serious-looking person, round eyed and with a heavy mustache. After a short inspection he nodded and turned to the driver.

"Take him to the doctor, Pete."

"You go along, Sheriff?" asked the driver.

"No, I can't. I'm right in a big pot. See yuh later."

He turned and hurried back across the street, while the stage went on down to the doctor's home.

Doctor Henry answered their knock, arrayed in a nightgown and a blanket, and told them to bring the man into the house.

An examination showed that the young man had been shot through the left shoulder, and that the bullet was still in him. He had lost considerable blood, but the doctor assured them that the wound was not necessarily fatal.

"I don't know him," replied the driver in answer to the doctor's questions. "He ride from Caliente. He say something 'bout San Francisco. He don't talk much. Maybe somebody know him here."

They left the doctor and went back. Pinnacle was beginning to wake up now. The driver let Hashknife and Sleepy have space in the stable for their horses, and offered them a bed at the rear of the stage office.

"That damned hotel no good," he told them. "Too much bug. You have good bed in my place — cost not'ing."

They thanked him kindly and accepted his offer. Hashknife's rheumatism was less painful now; and while Pinnacle awoke to the fact that the stage had been robbed and a man shot, Hashknife and Sleepy burrowed down in a fairly good bed and forgot that such things as wounded men and stage robbers ever existed.

CHAPTER
TWO

BIG MEDICINE HAWKWORTH

And at about the same time a cowboy bad brought a message to Big Medicine Hawkworth. He was one of Hawkworth's men, a thin, wry-necked cowboy, with badly bowed legs and bat ears.

The living-room of Hawkworth's home was almost a hovel. The ceilings sagged badly and every board in the bare floor creaked in a different key. One or two faded pictures hung askew on the walls, and in the center of the ceiling hung an old oil-burning chandelier with a cracked chimney and a badly bent reflector.

Near the center of the room, huddled in a striped blanket, sat Big Medicine Hawkworth, a veritable giant in stature, but as lean as a wolf. His big, bony head was covered with a huge mop of yellowish-white hair, which flared out from his ears, reaching to his cheekbones, and giving him the appearance of wearing crumpled horns.

His forehead was broad and high, his eyes set far apart and hidden beneath heavy brows. The nostrils of his finely chiseled nose flared out above a wide, heavy mouth, which sagged just enough to show a glimpse of heavy teeth. The lower jaw was firm, and perhaps a trifle belligerent.

Just now he humped in his chair, as if asleep, his huge hands gripping slightly at the blanket at his knees. The cowboy who had brought the message squatted on his heels beside the door, slowly rolling a cigarette.

A big black cat, its eyes glistening in the rays from the lamp, came in past the squatting cowboy, shrank quickly away from his reaching hand, darted across the room, and sprang onto the table near Big Medicine.

The stairs creaked noisily as another cowboy came down into the hall, carrying his boots. He was a stolid-faced, pudgy-looking person. His socks were not mates, and one of them was minus the whole toe. He peered into the sitting-room, nodded at the squatting cowboy.

Against the wall, beyond Big Medicine, was a cheap phonograph. The bootless cowboy deposited his boots in the hall, crossed the room over the protesting boards, and squatted down to put on a record.

Big Medicine did not look up. He knew that "Musical" Matthews had come down the stairs, and was going to play something on the phonograph before breakfast. He had been doing the same thing before breakfast for five years.

From the kitchen came breakfast odors, the rattle of dishes, the unmistakable rattle of stove lids. From somewhere outside the house came the sound of a man's voice raised in song:

I'll saddle my pony and feed him some ha-a-a-ay;
And I'll buy me a bottle to drink on the wa-a-ay.

14

Big Medicine lifted his head slightly, as the phonograph scratched and spluttered the opening of "The Holy City." He had heard it every morning for five years — or one just like it. It was Musical Matthews' favorite.

In fact it was the only one Musical Matthews played. He sat entranced until the last notes of the singer faded out in a splutter, like someone frying eggs in a hot pan. Then he got up, crossed the creaking floor to his boots, which he drew on slowly, and went out to the wash bench, where the other singer was washing his face and hands.

Big Medicine lifted his head and looked at the cowboy squatting at the door.

"The stage was held up, was it? And a man shot?"

"That's what I heard," replied the cowboy. "The sheriff came back to the poker game and told us. He didn't know how much they got, nor he didn't know how bad hurt this man was."

Big Medicine nodded slowly and shifted his hands.

"And these two strange men, Ike. What did they look like?"

"I didn't see 'em close, boss. One was tall and kinda limped; the other wasn't so tall."

"All right, Ike."

The cowboy uncoiled and clumped outside. Big Medicine took a crumpled letter from inside his blanket and looked at it. The cowboy had brought it from Pinnacle. He seemed interested in a few lines, which read:

I am sending you the $20,000 by express, in a plain package. The valuation is just, enough to have it carried in their safe, but not enough to tempt anyone to steal it.

Big Medicine put the paper back into his shirt and closed his eyes again. The black cat seemed to ooze off the table onto his lap, and one of his big hands caressed its head. A door creaked open and an Indian woman came softly down the hall to the living-room door.

She was a big woman, past middle age, with the stolid features of her race. Her calico dress was ill-fitting, but clean. Big Medicine lifted his head and looked at her for a long time before he said.

"Somebody held up stage last night, Lucy."

The squaw merely stared at him unmoved.

"My money was on that stage," he told her. "It was much money — all we had. I was goin' to buy half of the Yellow King Mine with that money."

"From Jim Reed?" she asked.

"Yeah."

"No good. Jim Reed bad. You lose just same. Come and eat."

Big Medicine squinted at her for several moments before getting to his feet. He was so tall that he had to stoop under the hanging lamp.

"Lucy," he said, "there are times when I thank the good God that I have you instead of a white woman. You never complain, never nag; trust me implicitly, believe in your dumb way that what I do is best. By the gods, there are times when I thoroughly appreciate you, Lucy."

"Sometime — not so much," she said slowly.

Big Medicine reached up and turned down the big lamp, before following her out into the hall and down to the dining-room, which was a kitchen and dining-room combined.

A girl was standing at the stove, baking hot cakes, while Ike Marsh, Musical Matthews, and Cleve Davis, the singing cowpuncher, sat at the table, eating.

Big Medicine sat down at the head of the table, still wearing his blanket, and the girl came to him, carrying a platter heaped with steaming cakes. She was unmistakably a half-breed girl, but almost as white as Big Medicine; a tall, lithe, big-eyed girl, of about eighteen, with a long braid of raven hair thrown carelessly across one shoulder.

She was the daughter of Big Medicine and Lucy; half-English, half Nez Percé. Big Medicine had brought his squaw from the Northwest, and they had named the girl Kwann, which, in the trade language of the Northwest, means Glad. But she was known to everyone of Hawk Hole as Wanna.

Big Medicine did not realize that Wanna had suddenly grown from a gangling little girl to a handsome young lady; but Lucy knew it. She could tell it in the admiring glances of the cowboys when she and Wanna went to Pinnacle to trade; she could read it in the sidewise glances of Big Medicine's own cowboys, and from the fact that they were always ready to bring wood or water for the kitchen.

"I seen Torres in Pinnacle last night," offered Ike Marsh, his mouth filled with food. "Him and Luis Garcia comes into the Greenback Saloon."

Big Medicine's brows lifted slightly, but he did not comment on the appearance of two men he had ordered out of the country. Pedro Torres, or "Pete" as he was better known, was an unprincipled rascal, flashy dresser, handsome in a way, and too clever ever to make an honest living.

Luis Garcia was Pete's shadow; a low-caste, half-Mexican, half-Apache.

"I seen Jim Reed, too." Ike was willing to pass out all the information he had, regardless of its interest. "Jim had a drink with Torres."

"And how much did you lose?" asked Musical.

"Not a dern cent. I was in seventeen dollars and I cashed in seventy-three dollars and four bits."

"'Faro' Lannin' must be gittin' easy," grinned Cleve. "He never let me win that much."

"Faro wasn't playin'. 'Arkansas' Jones was runnin' the game."

Big Medicine looked up from eating, his deep-set eyes speculative.

"One of you boys go to Pinnacle and see how bad that feller was hurt," he ordered. "The other two of yuh take a swing back toward the Devil's Corral and look around."

The Devil's Corral was Big Medicine's appellation for the wire fence which indicated the boundary line between Mexico and the United States. Big Medicine had no use for a Mexican, and the brown men on, the opposite side of the line reciprocated, as far as Big Medicine was concerned.

"I'll go to town," said Ike, shoving back from the table.

"Sure yuh would," grinned Musical. "That seventy-three dollars is burnin' a hole in yore pocket."

"Nawsir!" Ike shook his head violently. "Lot of that is goin' into a new saddle — mebbe all of it. If I play a-tall, it'll be jist to see if I can't win enough to add a new pair of chaps, thassall."

"Kiss yore money good-bye," laughed Cleve. "It's fellers like you that buy diamonds for fellers like Faro Lannin'. C'mon, Musical."

They went outside, rattling their spurred heels on the rough boards. Lucy sat down at the table.

"Me and Wanna go to town bimeby," she said. "Grocery most all gone. You want somethin'?"

Big Medicine shook his head and got up from the table. Wanna came from the stove and gave her mother a cup of coffee. Then she left the room. Big Medicine looked after her, a quizzical expression in his eyes. He turned to see Lucy looking after Wanna.

"Wanna is gettin' to be a big girl," he said slowly.

Lucy looked up at him.

"Yeah — woman now."

"Eighteen," said Big Medicine softly. "Eighteen years old. She's pretty."

"She's half-breed, Big Medicine."

The big man turned his head slowly and looked toward the door where Wanna had made her exit.

"Half-breed," he muttered.

19

The squaw made a sucking noise as she drank coffee from her saucer.

"She marry greaser, Mexican, bad *hombre* some kind," said the squaw slowly.

There was no bitterness in her voice, but Big Medicine knew what was in her heart.

"Mebbe not, Lucy," he said. "Wanna is good girl."

"Mebbe not?" Lucy lowered her saucer and stared up at him. "You say that? Will a crow try to mate with an eagle, Big Medicine?"

He shifted his eyes from her face and looked away. She was but quoting his own words, words which had been spoken years before. But the squaw had not forgotten them.

"If the crow thinks he is an eagle," he said softly.

"Wanna knows."

Lucy got up from the table and began clearing away the dishes. Big Medicine watched her, leaning one big hand on the table. His blanket had fallen from his massive shoulders, exposing a torso that would have been a credit to any professional athlete. Perhaps age had slowed those rope-like muscles, but it had sapped little of their strength.

After a few moments he replaced his blanket and turned to the doorway.

"Wanna knows," repeated Lucy, as if to herself. "But she is only a squaw. Squaw don't count."

She did not look at Big Medicine, but busied herself at the stove. For several moments he looked at her, and seemed about to speak, but changed his mind. His blanketed shoulders shrugged slightly, as he turned, ducked his head and went back into the living-room, where the loose boards creaked under his heavy tread, and the rocking chair squeaked a protest when he sat down.

CHAPTER
THREE

TORRES TAKES A BATH

It was about noon when Hashknife and Sleepy awoke. Hashknife had slept well for the first time in several nights, but was still crippled. They dressed and went into the street. The stagedriver, Olsen, had slept in the same room with them, but had managed to dress without awakening them.

There was nothing pretentious about Pinnacle. In fact there was little excuse for its existence, except as an outfitting point for the Greenhorn Mines. The buildings were mostly of adobe, and none of them more than one story.

On the west side of the street were a blacksmith shop, stage station, post-office, two saloons, and a restaurant, while on the opposite side were two saloons, two stores, a hotel, and an assay office.

One of these saloons was the Greenback, which boasted a full assortment of gambling paraphernalia, a small dance-hall, and enough "girls" to make things interesting for the lonely miners or cowpunchers.

There were no sidewalks in Pinnacle. The more pretentious of the buildings had porches or wooden awnings, supported by rough posts, and practically every building had a long hitch-rack in front, making almost a continual railing on each side of the street.

Hashknife and Sleepy found the sheriff, Lon Pelly, in the one café, and he made room for them at his table, after introducing himself. Their names meant nothing to the sheriff, who asked them for an account of the holdup and shooting. He had already had a talk with the stagedriver.

"Got any idea who this young feller is?" asked Hashknife, after he had told what they knew about it.

The sheriff shook his head quickly.

"I dunno who he is. The doctor says he's goin' to live. He's conscious now."

"How much of a haul did they make, Sheriff?"

"Dunno that either. The way bills of the express company were in the treasure box, so they got the whole works. I don't reckon anybody'll know until the express company checks up on it."

"What gits me," observed Sleepy, "is why they shot that young feller. He didn't reach for no gun."

"Didn't, eh?"

"Hell, no! His hands were still in the air when he fell. It was a dirty deal, I tell yuh."

"Don't tell," cautioned the sheriff. "Pinnacle is a place where folks with soft, voices live longer than yelpers. No offense, my friend — just be cautious; sabe?"

"Thanks," grunted Sleepy, and attacked his ham and eggs.

"This ain't the county seat, is it?" asked Hashknife.

"This place?" The sheriff grinned. "Caliente is the county seat. Me and my deputy been back in the Greenhorn country on a case. Don't get in here very often. Pinnacle ain't favorable to sheriffs."

A man came in and looked owlishly around. He was as tall as Hashknife, with a long, thin face, wispy mustache, which grew heavier on one side than the other, faded blond hair, and a nose that had been, at some time, knocked slightly out of plumb with the rest of his features.

He goggled at the sheriff, grinned widely, and pointed at him with a shaking finger.

"There y'are, li'l angel," he gurgled. "Hol' still, now."

He came slowly across the room and almost fell over the table in seating himself. The sheriff grunted disgustedly, and it irritated the tall one.

"Ain't I good enough t' set here?" he asked indignantly. "Whazza matter 'ith me, I'd crave t' know. Yesshir, I'd crave a li'l information, tha's what I'd crave."

"Yo're goin' to crave a punch in the nose, if yuh don't sober up," declared the sheriff.

"Thasso?"

The tall one looked drunkenly at Hashknife and Sleepy. Satisfied with his inspection he turned back to the sheriff.

"My God, Lonnie, yuh wouldn't jump on to me, wouldja?" he asked tearfully. "I'm one of yore mos' val'able friends. I'd do anythin' for you, Lonnie — you sawed-off, hat-eared, bug-headed cross between a —

24

Lonnie, I like you, and yore cruel words cuts me to the quick, that's what they do."

"Yeah, I'll betcha."

The sheriff turned and introduced his deputy, "Cloudy" Day, to Hashknife and Sleepy.

"He ain't worth a damn to me," declared the sheriff. "I dunno how I stand for him. He keeps sober in Caliente, 'cause he's got a wife that whales hell out of him for drinkin'; but when he gits up here he forgets her."

"Noshir." Cloudy shook his head. "Ain't true. I defy myshelf to get that drunk, and I ain't curshed with a big mem'ry. My wife is a shister of our estimable sheriff, and" — Cloudy grinned widely — "if he didn't give me a job, he'd have to board both of us; so he makes me earn m' keep."

"Lot of truth in that, too," agreed the sheriff.

They left Cloudy trying to decide what to eat, and went to the Greenback Saloon. A few miners had come in from the camp at Greenhorn and were trying to beat one of the roulette wheels, but outside of that there was little going on there.

Ike Marsh was at the bar, talking to Faro Lanning, the owner of the Greenback. Lanning was a typical gambler, even to the waxed black mustache and the diamond horseshoe in his shirt bosom. He nodded to the sheriff, gave Hashknife and Sleepy a sharp glance, and turned back to the bar.

After the trio passed, he turned again and looked quizzically at Hashknife's limping gait. Further back in the room, Torres and Garcia sat at a little table, Garcia asleep, while Torres perused a Mexican newspaper. At sight of Hashknife and Sleepy, Torres tapped Garcia on the ankle with the toe of his polished boot, and the half-breed looked quickly around.

The sheriff wandered over to the roulette wheel, while Hashknife and Sleepy sat down at a table. A man came in from the rear, and passed them on his way to the bar; a portly, well-dressed Chinaman. He gave them a keen glance, as he passed, and went to the bar.

"No pokah today, Faro?" he asked, smiling broadly.

"Hello, Lee."

Faro removed his cigar and motioned the Chinaman to have a drink with him.

"No poker," he replied. "Nobody wants to play, I guess."

Torres and Garcia left their table and came past the bar, heading for the front door.

"Want to play pokah, Torres?" asked the Chinaman.

"Not today," said the Mexican with hardly an accent. "Little too early, anyway. Later, perhaps."

They went on outside, and Faro and the Chinaman turned back to their drinks.

"What do yuh think of this place?" asked Sleepy.

"Kinda peculiar," smiled Hashknife softly. "Them two at the bar are wonderin' who we are, and that flashy-lookin' Mexican woke his partner up to take a look at us."

"I've got a hunch that a Sunday School wouldn't do very much business in Pinnacle, Sleepy; but that ain't none of our business. I reckon we'll saddle up and hunt for them hot springs pretty soon. That stagedriver

26

scared a lot of rheumatism out of me last night, but most of it's comin' back."

The sheriff left the roulette game and came back to them.

"Do you know where the hot springs are?" asked Sleepy.

"Hot springs? You mean the ones out at the Hawkworth ranch?"

"That's the ones."

"Yeah, I can tell yuh how to get there. It's only two miles. Do you know Big Medicine Hawkworth?"

"Never heard of him until last night," replied Hashknife. "They tell us the water is good for rheumatism."

"Yeah? Well, I suppose it is. Big Medicine is a queer sort of a jigger. He don't hardly leave the ranch. Ain't been out of Hawk Hole for twenty-five years, they tell me. Mebbe he'll let yuh bathe in his hot water, and mebbe he won't.

"He owns most of Hawk Hole, yuh see. Owns about all the water, and nobody can range cattle here, except him. Had kind of a little kingdom of his own, until the Greenhorn Mines opened up and made an excuse for this town.

"Some of the boys say that the Hawkworth ranch is haunted. The old house, creaks all over, and there's black cats by the dozen, so they tell me. I dunno anythin' about it. I do know that he's got three cowpunchers that'll fight anythin'. That was one of 'em at the bar when we come in. Name's Ike Marsh."

"Ain't there any other cattle ranches in here?" asked Hashknife.

"Not in the Hole. East of here is the K-10 outfit. They're runnin' cattle in the hills. 'Baldy' Kern owns it. Baldy has six punchers with his outfit, and they ain't shrinkin' vi'lets, but he keeps his stock out of the Hole. Hawkworth don't seem to be tryin' to get rich. Ever' so often he runs a few head of stock out to Caliente, sells 'em to a buyer there, and that's all.

"I reckon he's satisfied to set at home and kinda let the world alone. 'Tsall right, if yuh like it thataway. Ho hum-m-m-m" — he yawned widely — "I reckon I'll find Cloudy and start for home. Long ways to Caliente. If yuh want to go to Hawkworth's ranch, ride out the same way yuh came in last night. About a quarter of a mile out of town, take the road to the left."

The sheriff drifted away, and Hashknife and Sleepy went outside. An old, dilapidated buckboard drawn by two gray horses, came into the street and drew up in front of a store. In it were Lucy and Wanna. Torres and Garcia were just coming out of the store as they drove up to the hitch-rack, and Torres hurried out to tie the horses for them.

Hashknife and Sleepy sauntered down the street, passing the hitch-rack and getting their first glance at the feminine members of the Hawkworth household. Hashknife looked sharply at the older woman. He was familiar with the tribes of the Northwest, and it seemed homelike to see a familiar face again.

Torres was talking to Wanna, who turned away from him and looked at Hashknife. He had seen many

28

half-breed girls, but none so pretty as Wanna Hawkworth. Lucy spoke sharply to the girl and started for the store; but Torres laughed and tried to detain Wanna.

"Let her go," said Torres not unpleasantly. "It's been a long time since I had a chance to talk to you, Wanna."

"You no talk now," said Lucy flatly. "Come, Wanna."

The girl started to walk around Torres, but the Mexican again blocked her. He seemed so persistent in forcing his attentions upon her that Hashknife stopped and walked toward them. The girl looked at Hashknife, who limped up within a few feet of Torres.

Garcia had halted near the end of the hitch-rack, rolling a cigarette, and evidently enjoying the scene — until Sleepy moved in beside him, resting one arm on the top pole of the rack and squinting into the half-breed Apache's face.

Torres turned his head and looked at Hashknife, and as he did so, Wanna stepped past him and hurried to join her mother. Torres' face flushed slightly, and his eyes narrowed.

"I just wondered," said Hashknife slowly, half-apologetically, "if you had a match, pardner."

Torres' hand went to his pocket, but came away empty. He realized that Hashknife did not want a match. He turned his head and looked at Garcia, who was scowling at Sleepy.

"You want a match, eh?" said Torres slowly. "My friend, I am very sorry, but I have none."

"Thassall right," said Hashknife. "Much obliged just the same."

He walked past Torres and went into the store, followed by Sleepy, who was grinning widely. Torres scowled heavily and looked at Garcia.

"Who are these men?" demanded Torres in Spanish.

"How should I know?" replied Garcia heavily. "I did not speak to the pig who grins only with his mouth."

"They are strangers here," mused Torres. "Last night they came on the stage."

"This morning," corrected Garcia. "They were talking with the sheriff, who is also a fool."

"A fool is one who thinks that others do not have brains," rebuked Torres. "A wise man overrates his opponent."

This was a trifle beyond the mentality of Garcia, but he nodded violently, being of an agreeable disposition.

Hashknife and Sleepy went into the general store, where Lucy and Wanna were at a counter buying groceries. The girl glanced sharply at them, but the old squaw gazed upon them frankly. She realized that they had saved Wanna from an embarrassing situation, and she was grateful.

"*Klahowya*," said Hashknife, smiling.

The old squaw opened her mouth twice before she replied with the same word. It was the universal greeting used by both whites and Indians where she had been raised, and it had been many years since she had heard it spoken.

For several moments she seemed deep in thought. Then —

"*Mah-sie*," she said softly.

30

It had been difficult for her to remember "Thank you" in that language.

Hashknife smiled and shook his head. Wanna was staring at him now. She did not understand the language. Hashknife and Sleepy purchased some tobacco and left the store, going over to the stage stable, where their horses had been put up.

"You made a hit with the old squaw," grinned Sleepy. "By golly, she sure grinned a heap. But, honest to grandma, didja ever see a prettier half-breed girl, Hashknife?"

"For once in my life, I've got to agree with yuh," grinned Hashknife. "She's pretty. It seems kinda funny to see a *klooch* from the Northwest down in this country. She's as far away from home as we are, and she's been away a long time, too. It took her a long time to remember the jargon. I reckon she's a Nez Percé or a Nespelem. Mebbe Flathead."

"Somethin' like that," agreed Sleepy as they saddled. "Anyway, that *tenas kloochman* shore, is pretty. A reg-lar Minnehaha Laughin' Water."

Hashknife turned from fastening a *latigo* and squinted at his partner.

"Aw, I know my loop's draggin'," grinned Sleepy. "Yuh don't need to chide me, tall feller. Dang yuh, can't I admire beauty if I want to? I've got eyes and a heart."

"Yeah," drawled Hashknife. "When they passed around eyes and hearts yuh robbed the platter, but when the brains came you was all filled up. Git yore thoughts off beauty and kinda concentrate on my rheumatism. That's what we came here for."

"That's right, Hashknife. We've got to get you cured up, even if the pretty girls do show up to take my mind off yore aches."

They led their horses back to the street through the alley between the stage station and the post-office. Torres was standing between them and the door of the post-office, looking intently at the door. He did not hear the two men and horses come out of the alley.

Three riders were coming in from the east, their horses drifting along slowly. Then the post-office door opened and Wanna came out, followed closely by Lucy. With an exaggerated bow, Torres swept off his sombrero. Lucy grasped Wanna by the arm, as if to turn her in the opposite direction, but Torres stepped in quickly and spoke to them.

His attitude was entirely apologetic, but his words were probably not, judging from the expression on the old squaw's face. Hashknife dropped his reins, and in three long strides had reached Torres. His right hand caught the slack seat of Torres' trousers, while his left twisted into the gorgeous silk muffler.

Torres ripped out an expressive Spanish oath, as his hands tried to draw a weapon, but Hashknife swung him aloft, whirled on his heels and fairly ran to the blacksmith shop, a short distance away, where the worthy smith was fitting shoes on a bad horse, and dumped the luckless Mexican headfirst into a very dirty slack tub.

This tub was made from a half-barrel, and was nearly full of inky water. The three riders whirled their horses up to the front of the shop and fairly fell out of their saddles. Sleepy had dropped the two sets of reins and was at the door of the shop ahead of the three men, as if to stop them, from any interference.

The immersion of Torres seemed of great satisfaction to the blacksmith, whose buffalo-horn-like mustaches jiggled convulsively in a paroxysm of silent mirth. Hashknife knew just about how long a human being might safely be immersed; so he kept Torres under for the full limit, while the three riders, blocked from an entrance by Sleepy, who was willing to forego the pleasure of watching the ducking to prevent interference, grinned widely.

Torres was far from being gaudy when Hashknife drew him out, half-drowned, and sat him against the forge to recover. Several other men, attracted by those at the entrance, came to see what was going on. Faro Lanning was one of these.

Torres' chin, which dripped dirty water and iron particles was buried in the bosom of a once-ornate silk shirt, but now a dirty brown, as he wheezed audibly to draw air into his lungs. He was far from dead, but too watersoaked to care what went on around him.

Hashknife walked back to the door. The three riders looked him over critically, but said nothing.

"What was the matter?" asked Lanning, jerking his thumb in the general direction of Torres.

Hashknife squinted thoughtfully at Torres and back at Lanning.

"He forgot, I reckon."

"Forgot what?"

"Forgot that I asked him for a match."

Lanning scowled after Hashknife and Sleepy, who were heading for their horses, and turned to the three men who had ridden in.

"Do you know what it was all about?" he asked.

"No-o-o," drawled one of the men. " We didn't see that anythin' was wrong, until this tall puncher had Torres in both hands and was packin' him like a flag. He shore is deliberate, that feller. Haw, haw, haw, haw!"

Torres managed to get back to his feet and was clinging to the anvil. His eyes were red from the dirty water and he was altogether mad, but his lips shut firmly as he looked at the crowd in front of the wide doorway.

"Kinda looks like it was goin' to be a wet season," remarked the smaller of the three cowboys humorously.

He was a thin-faced, sallow-looking person, and as he removed his big hat to wipe the perspiration from the sweatband, he exposed a head which was totally bald. The sallow skin of his head seemed to be stretched so tightly over his skull that it wrinkled slightly in the back of his neck, and there was a red circle around it, marking the line of his hat.

Taking him all in all, "Baldy" Kern was not a beautiful object. His teeth were bad, his boots bulged from bunions, and he did not conceal the fact that the law was something that concerned him not.

The other two cowboys laughed raucously at his witticism. Perhaps they were amused; perhaps they laughed because Baldy Kern had laughed. At any rate Torres' eyes flashed angrily as he lurched past them and out into the street, where he stopped and looked around, looking for the man who had almost drowned him.

Both Hashknife and Sleepy were already heading for the Hawkworth ranch, and the two men were just driving away from the hitch-rack farther up the street and across. Torres flapped his wet arms dismally and went stumbling across toward the Greenback Saloon.

"Who are them two strange punchers?" asked Kern.

Lanning did not know any more than Kern did, but he said "I dunno. They spent a lot of time with the sheriff, if that means anything to you, Kern."

After delivering this veiled information, Lanning went back up the street, leaving Kern to think it over.

"Didja hear about the holdup last night?" asked the blacksmith.

Kern looked up quickly. "What holdup?"

"Stage. Three men stuck her up back on the grades and swiped the treasure box. They shot a feller, too, a passenger. Didn't kill him."

"Who is he?" asked Kern.

"I dunno, Baldy. Stranger around here. Them two punchers was on the stage. Wounded man is down at the doctor's house."

Kern squinted thoughtfully over this information. Then —

"How much of a haul did they git?"

"I dunno."

It seemed a stock phrase with the blacksmith.

"Who was drivin' the stage — Olsen?"

"Yeah."

"Why did they shoot this stranger?"

"I dunno. Somebody said he went for his gun, but one of them punchers said it was a lie, that his hands were still in the air when he went down."

"Kinda queer," said Kern thoughtfully.

He shrugged his thin shoulders and went back to his horse. They crossed to the Greenback Saloon hitch-rack, and the blacksmith went back to work, grinning to himself. He did not like Torres.

Sleepy wore a wide grin as they rode away from Pinnacle but Hashknife's face was serious. The incident had not seemed as humorous to him as it had to Sleepy.

"I ain't laughin' at that gaudy Mexican's bath," explained Sleepy. "I'm grinnin' to think that you even forgot to limp."

"Eh?" Hashknife looked up quickly and a grin twisted his lips. "By golly, that's right. I plumb forgot to limp. And that only goes to show that most of these diseases are all in yore head. I was plumb lame until I seen that feller tryin' to talk to the women, and then I forgot all about it. Right now it's commencin' to hurt me, 'cause I'm thinkin' about it."

"You sure gave that Mexican a coolin'-off, cowboy. He jist sizzled. I didn't see it all, 'cause them three fellers rode up kinda fast, and I thought mebbe they was goin' to try and stop yuh. I dunno why it is" — Sleepy's tone changed and he became mournful — "it

36

seems like when there's any heroin' to be done I have to hold the horses."

Hashknife laughed, as he sifted a cigarette paper full of Durham.

"I wasn't tryin' to be a hero, Sleepy."

"You don't have to try" — mournfully — "it just comes kinda natural for you to do things like that. If I had tried it, I'd probably stubbed my toe before I got to him. Mebbe I'd 'a' got a few inches of steel in my anatomy and had to kill him."

"Mebbe I'll get a few inches of his steel yet," mused Hashknife. "He don't look like a feller that would take a baptisin' in a slack tub and jist grin."

"Mebbe yuh will, tall feller. Life's a queer thing, ain't it? Here we come into this country to try and soak out a case of rheumatism; jist a harmless occupation. The first thing we do is to run into a holdup and a shootin' scrape."

"Well, that's all right, Sleepy."

"No, it ain't." Sleepy spoke with conviction. "It ain't noways all right. I can see yore nose twitchin' and yore ears hang down like the ears of a pointer dog or a bloodhound. It ain't all right, I tell yuh. It ain't none of our business."

"Well," laughed Hashknife, "what about it?"

Sleepy sighed and shifted himself.

"What about it? Hashknife, you know danged well what about it. Ever since I can remember, me and you have been gettin' off to just this kind of a start. Trouble hunts us, I tell yuh."

"And you shake hands with it like it was a long-lost brother," grinned Hashknife. "If yo're born to be hung, you'll never choke to death on a fishbone, Sleepy."

"All right," nodded Sleepy. "Just the same, I wish we wasn't here. Mebbe we can get the aches soaked out of you before they start heavin' lead at us. We don't *sabe* these folks down here. Likely got a lot of smart gunmen, too."

"Well, old pessimist, we won't even stop at the Hawkworth ranch," decided Hashknife seriously. "If yore so scared of trouble, we'll go right on. My rheumatism is a lot better, yuh know."

"No, we won't. We're goin' to get yuh fixed up, if we have to throw lead at every man in Hawk Hole. Just what do yuh reckon is wrong around here?"

Hashknife grinned under the shade of his wide sombrero and shook his head. He knew that Sleepy was not afraid of anything, and that he merely wanted an alibi to point back to, in case they got into serious trouble.

But Sleepy was right when he said that wherever they went trouble followed them. It seemed that Fate sent them from range to range to straighten out trouble. Time after time they brought peace to troubled cattle land, but they did not stay to enjoy the fruits of their labors. Something urged them to go on and on, always looking for the other side of the hill, and on the other side of the hill they found more trouble.

And in spite of the fact that they deplored their calling, both of them enjoyed it. They would not stay and enjoy the peace which they had brought. Always they rode on, looking for a place to settle down, where they might buy a little cattle outfit and live out their lives in peace; the end of the rainbow, which never would be found.

They were top-hand cowboys in every respect; gunmen, if you please, although neither of them could split a second on the draw, nor hit a dollar at forty paces. In fact they deplored their slowness with a gun, and assured each other that some day they would meet a regular gunman who would make them wish they had never worn a weapon.

It was Hashknife's brain that worked out their problems. He was able to see details that an ordinary man would miss, and he had an uncanny way of piecing things together until he was able to weave a net around a criminal that nothing could break.

Sleepy's mind did not travel fast enough to keep up with Hashknife, but he had an instinct that told him when to be ready for trouble to break; so between the two they had come practically unscathed from many a gun battle, where the souls of men had gone to their Maker with the reek of powder smoke on them.

All these things had made them fatalists, and to believe as Hashknife had said: "If yo're born to be hung, you'll never choke to death on a fishbone, Sleepy."

This was their belief, ingrained from many incidents, which proved their point — to them, at least.

CHAPTER
FOUR

SO DOES HASHKNIFE

Hawkworth's Tumbling H ranch buildings were not much to look at. They were situated at the mouth of a cañon which gave them a fair view of the broad expanse of Hawk Hole, and the elements had colored them until they blended into the gray of the landscape.

The ranch-house was a two-story, half-adobe, half-frame construction. The house had originally been a one-story adobe, but later a frame had been built upon the original, giving it the appearance of a shack that had been lifted by a mud upheaval.

Behind it and to the right was a one-story adobe stable and a pole corral, where several horses drowsed in the heat. To the left of the ranch-house was the little adobe blacksmith shop, and back of that, nearer the cañon, was the bathhouse.

There was a general air of don't-care-a-hang-how-we-look about the place. The front yard was a bare expanse of gravel and weeds, the fence fallen down in places. It might have well been a deserted ranch instead of what it was. Sleepy sniffed disgustedly, as they rode in past the sagging gate.

"For gosh' sake, what smells around here?" he asked.

"That's the hot springs," grinned Hashknife. "Sulphur and a lot of other stuff. I sabe the smell. Some folks like to drink it."

"Some folks ought to be investigated," grunted Sleepy. "You may lose yore rheumatism, but you'll gain somethin' worse. Git that stuff in yore hair and see how I stay around yuh."

A saddled horse was tied to a porch post, and as they dismounted its owner came out. And he stood not upon the order of his coming. The door had opened suddenly, and this man came out asprawl. He struck on his hands and knees at the edge of the top step, turned completely over, and landed out in the gravel.

He was a short, heavily built man of about forty years of age, with a reddish mustache and a florid complexion.

For several moments he blinked violently, got slowly to his feet, and walked over to his horse. He turned his head to stare at Hashknife and Sleepy, but lost no time in mounting his horse and riding away. His hat came out in the yard with him, but he did not stop to pick it up.

Hashknife and Sleepy grinned at each other, and turned toward the doorway to see Big Medicine Hawkworth looking at them. He was stooped in the doorway, his big hands hanging low, his mop of white hair falling forward over his eyes.

"What do you want?" he asked sullenly.

Hashknife grinned and looked toward the cloud of dust, which marked the passing of the man who had been thrown out.

"Not what he got," said Hashknife.

Big Medicine lifted his head and squinted down the road. His attention was attracted by the hat in the yard. Slowly he came down the steps, picked up the hat and sailed it far off across the tumbledown fence. Harshknife and Sleepy watched him with amusement as he came back to the edge of the porch.

"Perhaps," he said, "that was a childish thing to do, but I was irritated beyond endurance."

"Yeah," admitted Hashknife, "I reckon yuh was, pardner."

"Thank you," he said simply.

"I've got rheumatism," stated Hashknife, "and somebody said that yore hot spring was a sure cure. How about it?"

He considered the question gravely. "My dear man, there is no such a thing as a sure cure. It is all theory until proved by practice, and on each individual case. Diseases do not react the same in all bodies."

"You talk like a doctor," smiled Hashknife.

"I have studied," said Big Medicine slowly, pushing back the big mop of hair. "Perhaps I might better say, I have read."

"Outside of that," grinned Hashknife, "do I get to try out yore hot water?"

Big Medicine looked narrowly at Hashknife from under his bushy eyebrows for several moments. He seemed undecided. Then:

"I'm not in the habit of allowing strangers to use my spring, sir; but I should be a hell of a citizen if I refused to let a suffering man share what Nature provided. You

42

are welcome to use it as long as you find the need." He pointed to the rear of the ranch-house. "You will find the bathhouse back there, sir. I think your nose will guide you."

He smiled and walked back into the house, closing the door behind him.

"Can yuh beat that?" grinned Hashknife. "Looks like one of the old Bible prophets, talks like a dictionary, and throws men out through the front door. No wonder they say queer things about Big Medicine Hawkworth. Let's find the bathhouse."

Big Medicine was correct when he said that their noses would guide them. A cloud of vapor was coming from the adobe bathhouse, and with it the odor that resembled that of decayed eggs.

Inside the place they found a six-by-nine sunken tub, made from rough boards, with an inlet and outlet made of square wooden pipe. Hashknife lost no time in undressing and getting into the tub. The water was almost too hot for comfort, but he was game to give it a trial.

Sleepy moved just outside the door to get away from the steam, and saw Lucy and Wanna drive up to the stable, where Ike Marsh met them and took charge of the team. They did not look toward the bathhouse as they crossed the yard and entered the kitchen door.

Hashknife spent about fifteen minutes in the tub, then dressed and came outside. The heat of the bath had weakened him, and he looked solemnly at Sleepy.

"If you'd stick a fork in me, you'd sure find me well done," he declared shakily. "There's parts of me that are kinda rare yet, I suppose, but another stewin' like that would sure put me in the fried egg class."

"Yuh look kinda shriveled up," admitted Sleepy, looking him over closely. "I seen a dead fish that looked like you. I'll betcha you'll start fallin' apart as soon as yuh get into the saddle ag'in, so I'll ride behind yuh and pick up the pieces."

They went back to their horses and started to mount, when Big Medicine came out to them.

"Where are yuh goin'?" he asked.

"Back to town," said Hashknife. "Thank yuh very much for the bath."

"You ain't goin' back to no town," declared Big Medicine. He was talking cow-town English now. "Yo're goin' to wrap up in a blanket and take a sleep. How in hell do yuh expect that hot bath to do yuh any good thataway? Yore pores are all open now, and if you catch cold, you'll have pneumonia. C'mon in the house and I'll show yuh a bed."

He turned and stalked inside, leaving no course open to Hashknife and Sleepy except to follow him. He led them up the creaking stairs and into a bedroom.

"You flop into that bed," he ordered. "When yuh get in, I'll have Wanna bring yuh a hot drink."

He turned to Sleepy.

"Put yore horses in the stable. Ike Marsh is down there and he'll show yuh where to put 'em."

He went back down with Sleepy and they met Lucy and Wanna in the living-room. Big Medicine turned to Sleepy.

"I beg your pardon," he said slowly, "but I have never heard your name."

"My name's Stevens," smiled Sleepy. "My friends all call me Sleepy."

"Ah, yes." He turned to the women. "May I present Mr. Stevens? Mr. Stevens, this is my wife, Mrs. Hawkworth, and my daughter, Wanna."

The old squaw held out her hand.

"I like to meet you," she said. "How do?"

"Pleased to meetcha," grinned Sleepy, and held out his hand to Wanna. She shook hands shyly and moved back.

"His friend is upstairs in bed," said Big Medicine, looking at Wanna. "In about ten minutes, I want you to mix him a hot drink of rum, sugar, and water and take it up to him, Wanna."

The girl nodded quickly and went toward the kitchen. Big Medicine led Sleepy outside and pointed toward the corral, where Ike Marsh was repairing a broken pole.

"Take your horses down there, Mr. Stevens. Ike will show you where to put them."

"Thank yuh," nodded Sleepy, and went to get the animals.

Ike Marsh met him at the stable door and Sleepy told him Big Medicine's orders.

"Yeah, we got room," said Ike, opening the doors.

They put the animals in two vacant stalls and came outside. Sleepy passed his tobacco and papers and they squatted down to smoke.

"I seen you fellers go up to the bathhouse," said Ike thoughtfully, "and I wondered if you was friends of Big Medicine."

"We dunno yet," smiled Sleepy. "Yuh see, we never seen him before in our lives."

"Yuh didn't?"

Ike inhaled deeply at the wonder of it all.

"Yuh never seen him before, eh? Well, I'll just say that yo're lucky, if yuh needed a hot bath. Big Medicine ain't in the habit of lettin' strangers use his private tub. Yuh see, he's got an idea that somebody might beat him out of the spring."

"Is it worth anythin'?" asked Sleepy.

"Hell, I dunno." Ike wrinkled his nose. "Not to me, it ain't. I've been here a long time, but she still smells like hell. I suppose she's worth somethin'. I dunno. Goin' to stay long?"

Sleepy told him why they hadn't gone back to town.

"That makes me paw my head," declared Ike. "Mebbe you and yore pardner hypnotized Big Medicine."

"What kind of a feller is he?" asked Sleepy.

"Jist, what you've seen. He's two kinds of person if yuh know what I mean. Sometimes he gits dignified as a undertaker and talks like a book, and the next minute he talks like the rest of us. Who in hell was Shakespeare?"

"I dunno him," admitted Sleepy.

"Me neither. Big Medicine did. Hell, yeah! Repeats things that Shakespeare said. I don't *sabe* what it means, but it kinda pleases Big Medicine; so we listen.

Oh, he's smart, all right. And if yuh don't think he'll fight, try him."

"I'll take yore word for it," grinned Sleepy. "He threwed a man out just as we rode up."

Ike grunted softly and looked at Sleepy.

"He did?"

"Him, or somebody else in the house," nodded Sleepy. "Anyway, this feller sure came out all spraddled, town."

"That was Jim Reed," stated Ike wonderingly. "Wasn't nobody else but Jim Reed. He showed up when me and Big Medicine was talkin', so I came down here to the barn. Well, I'll be darned! Threwed him plumb out, eh?"

"Right on his neck."

"Uh-huh. Well, well! Him and Jim Reed was good friends."

"I'll betcha," grinned Sleepy. "He must 'a' jist loved old Jim."

"It shore has the earmarks of brotherly love," grinned Ike. "I don't like Jim Reed. He's from Greenhorn. Owns some mines, and I reckon he's been tryin' to peddle part of 'em to Big Medicine. How did yore pardner like his bath?"

"All right, I reckon. Big Medicine made him come in and go to bed. He's had rheumatism pretty bad, and we came here to see if the springs would cure it, yuh see. He was almost cured today. Got peeved at a gaudy-lookin' Mexican and threwed him into the slack tub in the blacksmith shop. Plumb forgot his limp."

"Th'owed a gaudy-lookin' Mex into a slack tub?" wondered Ike. "Had a little mustache, wore his hair long in front of his ears and dressed like a tin-horn gambler?"

"That's the curio," nodded Sleepy. "Wore a red sash instead of a belt."

"Pete Torres, as sure as the Devil made little apples. Th'owed him into a tub of dirty water! What did Pete do?"

"He damn near drowned. When we rode away he was braced ag'in' the forge, drippin' rusty water. I'll tell a man, he wasn't noways gaudy then."

"Aw gosh, that sounds too good to be true. I'd give half of my life to 'a' seen it done. Now listen: Tell yore pardner to look out for Torres. He's a bad *hombre*. What he don't know about th'owin' a knife ain't to be learned. Why, that son of a gun, could pin yore ears to the wall plumb across a room, and he's no slouch with a gun.

"And he's got a pardner named Garcia, half-Mex, half-Apache. If Tores asked Garcia to kill somebody, Garcia'd do it. He ain't got brains enough to see farther than the killin'. It won't be a even break, and yuh can bet on that."

"We're much obliged," said Sleepy sincerely. "Hashknife Hartley don't ask for a even break. That's my pardner's name. Mine's Sleepy Stevens."

"Mine's Ike Marsh."

They shook hands solemnly.

"Pleased to meetcha," said Sleepy.

"Happy t' know yuh," muttered Ike. "You fellers ain't from down in this country, are yuh? Notice yore boots are higher than most punchers wear down here."

"Got these in Miles City, Montana," said Sleepy.

"Hell, you fellers are shore travelers. Way up there, eh? I've heard about the cow-country up thataway. Good riders up there, they tell me. A Oregon puncher was a-tellin' me that the bronc-riders are better up there, and the horses bigger, but he said that the Southwest puncher was a better roper. I dunno."

"Mebbe" — Sleepy passed his Durham and papers — "I ain't seen enough punchers in this country to see how they compare. We've got some *hy-iu* cowhands up there, pardner. Where is that Oregon puncher?"

"Works for the K-10 outfit. Name's Sam Blair. I dunno just where he's from, but he talks about Oregon; so I figured he was from there."

"Uh-huh." Sleepy squinted away from the smoke of his cigarette and considered his toes. "What kind of an outfit is this K-10?"

"Cattle. Baldy Kern owns the place. Him and Big Medicine ain't friendly. Yuh see, Big Medicine didn't want another cattle outfit in Hawk Hole; so Baldy kinda sets on the edge. No, they ain't never had no open trouble, but Baldy knows where to head in at."

"Hawkworth been here a long, time, ain't he?"

"Hell, yes. Must 'a' come here twenty-five years ago. Took up a homestead, I reckon. Then he got other men to take up homesteads and turn 'em over to him. Bimeby he's got most of Hawk Hole. Then he bought the rest from the Government for about two bits per acre.

"I dunno what he wants it for. There's just him and Lucy and Wanna. Big Medicine ain't never been out of here since he came. Money don't mean nothin' to him. Once in a while we herds some cattle out to Caliente, sells 'em to a buyer, and Big Medicine shoves the money in his sock. Me and Musical and Cleve takes 'em out and brings back the money."

"Kind of a funny way to live," observed Sleepy. "His money don't do him much good. That half-breed girl is kinda pretty."

Ike ground his cigarette under his heel and got to his feet.

"She's a real nice girl," he said slowly, "and nobody ain't allowed to think any other way around here, Stevens."

"I didn't say nothin' wrong, did I?" asked Sleepy.

"No, yuh didn't. I don't think yuh had any idea of sayin' anythin' wrong, but I just wanted yuh to know how things lay."

"Suits me," smiled Sleepy. "Where I come from we ain't in the habit of sayin' anythin' against any girl, Marsh."

Ike considered it gravely and nodded. "That's a good country, Stevens. Let's go up to the house."

CHAPTER
FIVE

MOONLIGHT IN THE
BORDER COUNTRY

Pedro Torres was in a bad frame of mind over his enforced bath in the blacksmith shop. He made a few purchases at one of the stores, bought a bath in the one tub at the hotel, and became presentable again.

But his vanity had been badly injured, and he swore dire threats toward the man who had insulted him. He assured himself that he had done nothing wrong, merely desiring to talk with a half-breed girl.

Garcia was not sympathetic. He had seen the incident, and the fact that Torres hankered for revenge made little difference to Garcia. If Torres had asked Garcia to kill Hashknife, Garcia would have instantly agreed to do it.

Baldy Kern smiled grimly and polished his head. He was curious to know a few things about Hashknife and Sleepy. Baldy was not talkative, so he chose to listen. Cloudy Day, still full of liquor, had been told of the incident, and imagined that he had seen it.

"It sure was good," he announced in the Greenback Saloon. "That tall puncher was all crippled up with rheumatism, but he picked Torres up just like Torres wasn't nothin'. If that feller's got rheumatism, I'm paralyzed, thassall."

Baldy grinned widely. He had seen no evidences of Hashknife's being a cripple.

"Who is this feller, Cloudy?" he asked.

"Tha's a question," said Cloudy owlishly. "Lon introduced me to them, but I didn't git the names."

"Lon knows 'em, does he?"

"Oh, abs'lutely. Why, Lon's an old friend of theirs."

Baldy accepted this with a grain of salt. He knew that Cloudy was prone to exaggerate, especially when drinking; so he found Lon Pelly in the Yellow Stamp Saloon, bought Lon a drink, and swung the conversation around to the baptism of Torres.

Lou hadn't see it either.

"Must be strong," commented Baldy. "Torres ain't no little kid. They tell me that this stranger picked Torres up and packed him to the blacksmith shop."

"He's tall, but don't look very strong," said Lon. "I dunno anythin' about him, except what I got from talkin' with him a little. They was on the stage when it was held up. The tall one said they was goin' over to Hawkworth's for him to take baths for his rheumatism."

"Must be badly crippled," mused Baldy aloud.

"He did limp a little," offered Lon. "Mebbe he got so mad at Torres that he forgot to limp. A feller over in the restaurant seen it, and he said that Torres was bowin' and scrapin' to Wanna Hawkworth when this feller picked him up."

Baldy smiled softly and bought another drink. Did Lon know what this tall feller's name was?

"Name's Hartley. Short one is Stevens."

Baldy considered the names, but they meant nothing to him.

"How much of a haul did the robbers get?" he asked.

"Nobody seems to know," replied Lon.

"Got any idea who done it, Lon?"

"Yeah — three men."

Baldy left the Yellow Stamp and went down to the doctor's house. He had known Doctor Henry for several months. The doctor was an oldish man, very methodical, reserved.

"The patient is doing very nicely," he told Baldy. "I recovered the bullet, and can see no reason why, with proper care, he should not completely recover."

"That's fine," agreed Baldy. "Yo're some doctor. What was the feller's name, Doc?"

"His name is Jack Hill, I believe."

"Uh-huh. Jack Hill. Must be a stranger, eh?"

"I think he is, Mr. Kern. He is not inclined to talk about himself. My worry now is to get a suitable nurse for him. He says he is able to pay for services, and wants to be sent out, but such a thing would be impossible."

"I dunno where you'd find a nurse, Doc. Wimmin ain't noways plentiful around here, not the nursin' kind."

Baldy went back to the Greenback Saloon, none the wiser for his interviews.

He did not know anyone by the name of Jack Hill, and he wondered why the holdup man had shot him down. For his own satisfaction, Baldy desired to know things.

It was shortly after dark that Torres and Garcia mounted their horses and rode out of Pinnacle, heading south. Across the border was the Rancho Sierra, owned by Steve Guadalupe, who bred gamecocks and trouble. Steve was an old man and full of iniquity, who pointed with pride to the fact that his ancestors were, pure Castilian, when, as a matter of fact, he was a mixture of Portuguese, Mexican, and Yaqui.

Torres and Garcia were friends of Steve, as were most of the denizens of the border, whose deviltry served to bring dishonor upon the Mexicans as a people. The Rancho Sierra was too isolated for the Mexican Government to bother with Steve's doings, and the United States officers could only patrol the border and hate him from afar.

Two more of Baldy's men, Sam Blair and Jack Baum, had ridden into town just before Torres and Garcia rode away. Blair was a blocky-faced individual, none too intelligent-looking and of rather unkempt appearance.

Baldy met him at the hitch-rack and whispered for him to follow Torres and see where he was going. Blair nodded and rode out of town a few minutes after Torres and Garcia. Blair did not ask questions; neither did Baldy tell him why he wanted Torres followed.

It was one of those moonlight nights down in the border country, when the moon seems to almost rest upon the hills and bathes the world in a blue light. Blair had no difficulty in following Torres and Garcia. They rode slowly toward the south until a mile out of town, when they turned northeast, circling back around Pinnacle.

Blair waited until they had made their swing before following them. He rode a gray horse, which made him almost invisible in the gray blue of the landscape. Torres and Garcia rode faster now, keeping off the road and heading, straight for Hawkworth's. Tumbling H Ranch. Blair suspected that this was their goal, so he moved closer.

They swung wide of the ranch buildings and came in behind the stable, while Blair dismounted farther up the cañon and came down on foot. Two of the ranch-house buildings were illuminated, and he could hear a squeaky phonograph playing a waltz.

Blair came in behind the stable, going softly. He knew that Torres and Garcia were not far away. He crawled through the corral fence, went slowly along the side of the stable and out through the other side of the corral.

There was still no sign of Torres and Garcia. Blair peered around the corner of the stable. He could see the door of the bathhouse, which was illuminated from a light within. From the ranch-house came the sound of muffled voices.

Blair scratched his nose and considered things. If someone came from the rear door of the ranch-house, they could see him. He did not like his position in the matter at all. Someone was moving around in the bathhouse, and now the occupant came out, carrying a lantern, which gave little light.

Blair flattened himself against the wall, between the corner, of the barn and the corral, peering around to see which way the lantern-bearer was going.

Then there came a dull thud, and the man with the lantern went down, throwing the lantern aside, but not extinguishing it. Blair jerked back. Torres and Garcia ran past him, going around the corner of the corral and out to their horses.

In another minute he heard them riding swiftly away. The phonograph had started another turn. Blair squinted thoughtfully as he peered out again. He could see the black bulk of the man on the ground, and the spluttering lantern near him.

Cautiously Blair stepped away from the corner and went swiftly over to the man, who was lying on his back. He picked up the lantern and stepped in close, throwing the beams of light into the face of the man on the ground.

For several moments Blair stared down at that face, oblivious to everything. He bent closer, holding the lantern on a level with his own face, as he peered into the features of the injured man. A voice spoke to him out of the darkness and he jerked upright still clutching the lantern.

It was late that evening when Musical Matthews and Cleve Davis rode in at the Tumbling H and met Hashknife and Sleepy. In a few short words Big Medicine told them that Hashknife and Sleepy would be with them until Hashknife's rheumatism had succumbed to the effect of the hot baths.

56

Hashknife had just got out of bed and was feeling better, but slightly weak. Lucy had told about Hashknife's encounter with Torres, and it seemed to please everyone except Hashknife. Big Medicine seemed a bit dubious over the outcome of it. "Watch that Mexican," he warned Hashknife. "He's a snake."

"I've made snakes bite themselves," grinned Hashknife.

"Didja ever see one of them knife-throwin' Mex handle his weapon?" asked Musical.

"No," Hashknife shook his head. "I don't *sabe* 'em much."

"Then look out for 'em. Knives don't make no noise. I'd shore rather face a six-gun than a knife, and either Torres or his dirty-face pardner, Garcia, can shore pin your ears back with a knife at twenty feet."

Lucy came to announce supper, and they all clattered to the table, except Hashknife.

"I've done lost my appetite," he told them. "Couldn't eat a thing, folks; so I reckon I'll take the lantern and go out to the bathhouse. Another good soakin' and a big sleep will put me in the saddle again."

Lucy secured the lantern for him and he went out through the kitchen, while the rest of them did ample justice to the culinary efforts of Lucy and Wanna, who waited on the table silently.

"We rode beyond the breaks," Musical told Big Medicine. "As far as we can see, everythin' is all right. There wasn't many cows over on that side. From up on that saw-tooth ridge yuh can almost see the Rancho Sierra."

Big Medicine nodded and turned to Sleepy.

"This Rancho Sierra is across the border. Belongs to old Steve Guadalupe, the meanest old Mexican that ever stole a cow. We have to keep our eyes open all the time, Stevens. They've raided us a few times."

"Yuh can't get 'em back after they cross the line, eh?"

"Not very well. Our business is to keep them far enough on this side to make it hard for them to grab Very many. Guadalupe has a tough gang down there, rustlers, smugglers, and all that kind of folks."

"I wonder if it was some of his gang that held us up the other night," said Sleepy.

Big Medicine frowned heavily, but said nothing.

"Hell, you don't have to go into Mexico to find holdup men," said Cleve Davis. "There's plenty of 'em on this side of the line. I've got a hunch that it was white men from this side of the line that stole the last bunch of cattle from us."

"That K-10 outfit?" began Musical, but Big Medicine stopped him with a gesture.

"Name no names, Musical, please," he said softly. "There is bad blood between this ranch and the K-10, and the least said the better. Give them the benefit of the doubt, until we are sure."

"All right, Big Medicine. I s'pose that's right, too. But I get kinda mad once in a while."

"You should learn to control your temper."

Sleepy grinned, as he remembered how Big Medicine had pitched Jim Reed out on his head that morning. Big Medicine had said nothing about being mad, but had admitted that Reed had irritated him beyond endurance. Sleepy wondered what Big Medicine might do if he became mad.

They finished their meal and went back to the creaky-floored living-room, where Musical proceeded to put a record on the phonograph. After the second record Sleepy grew nervous. He hitched his chair around, tore up two cigarette papers, and decided he would go and see how Hashknife was getting on with his bath.

He went out through the kitchen, where. Lucy and Wanna were clearing off the table, and the old squaw handed him a clean towel.

"I ain't goin' to take a bath," he told her smiling.

"All right. You giveum to tall man. He need much towel."

"There is quite a lot of him," grinned Sleepy. "Thanks."

The door was not latched and he stepped out softly. The bathhouse was only fifty feet away. About ten feet from the open door of the bathhouse crouched a man, holding a lantern in such a way that his face was fully illuminated. Lying on the ground was the body of a man.

Sleepy stepped forward, his right hand reaching back to his gun.

"What are you doin' here?" he almost shouted.

Sam Blair jerked up, still holding the lantern, but flung it aside as he drew his gun. The lantern had barely smashed to the ground when the two men began shooting.

Sleepy felt the first bullet as it passed his head, and fired twice in rapid succession. Blair fired again, but the streak of flame from his guns was pointing upward and the bullet went streaking toward the North Star, while Blair stumbled and went down in a heap.

It was all over in five seconds. The kitchen door crashed open and the three cowpunchers, headed by Big Medicine, came running out. Sleepy was going toward Blair, covering him with his gun, when Big Medicine joined him.

"What happened?" he panted. "What was the matter?"

"Watch that jigger," said Sleepy hoarsely. "I think he's got Hashknife."

Sleepy fell on his knees beside Hashknife, while the others scratched matches. Big Medicine came from Blair.

"Take him into the house," he ordered. "This other feller ain't goin' to get away, until he's carried away."

They carried Hashknife into the house and placed him on the floor, while Big Medicine made a swift examination.

"He got hit, that's all," declared Big Medicine, pointing to an egglike swelling on Hashknife's head between his eye and ear. "He'll be all right in a few minutes, I think."

Sleepy sighed with relief and leaned against the wall.

"That other jigger opened the ball," he said wearily. "His first bullet almost creased me. He was humped over Hashknife, lookin' him over with a lantern, when I went out there. I just had a hunch that somethin' was wrong."

Big Medicine nodded slowly.

"It was Sam Blair of the K-10 outfit," he said softly.

"Dead?" asked Musical.

"Yes."

Musical shrugged his shoulders.

"The war is on, I reckon."

"Aw, that's too bad," said Sleepy. "Dang it, I had to shoot."

"Sure yuh did," assured Musical. "That's all right, Stevens."

The practical Lucy came in with a basin of water and a towel, with which she proceeded to bathe Hashknife's head and face. He opened his eyes and stared up at them in wonderment.

"How are yuh feelin', pardner?" asked Sleepy.

Hashknife sat up and felt gingerly of his head.

"What happened?" he asked foolishly.

"Somebody hit yuh when yuh came out of the bathhouse."

"Oh, yeah." Hashknife got to his feet and blinked painfully. "I remember startin' out, when somethin' hit me and I seen a million stars. Who was it, Sleepy?"

"I dunno."

Sleepy scratched his head nervously, as he told Hashknife what he had done.

"They tell me that his name was Sam Blair," said Sleepy.

"From the K-10 outfit," said Musical quickly. "Mebbe we better kinda look around with a lantern, eh?"

Hashknife and Sleepy exchanged a quick glance.

"You feel good now?" asked Lucy anxiously, dripping water from the towel and the basin.

"Yeah, I feel fine," lied Hashknife. "Ain't got a pain in either leg."

The boys had secured another lantern and were going out to look around. Hashknife sat down in a chair and Lucy proceeded to attack the swelling with compresses. In a few minutes Musical came hack and placed a long-bladed knife, with a horn handle, on the table beside Hashknife.

"There's what hit yuh," he declared. "Whoever throwed it at yuh must 'a' misjudged a little and hit yuh with the hilt. It was right near where yuh was layin'. And," added Musical, "that Sam Blair wasn't no knife-thrower."

"Wasn't he?"

Hashknife looked the knife over carefully. It was a wicked weapon, almost as sharp as a razor, and with a point like a needle. "Do yuh reckon the Mexican did it?" asked Hashknife.

"You'll probably never know who done it," said Ike. "Sam Blair is too dead to skin. Mebbe he knowed who threw it. If he didn't, what in hell was he doin' out there? Big Medicine swore he'd kill the first K-10 puncher that showed up; swore that to Baldy Kern.

"It's shore too bad, but it can't be helped. The K-10 will declare war as sure as hell. Not that we care a whoop what they do, except that it'll mean a killin'."

Ike turned to Sleepy.

62

"That Sam Blair is the puncher I was tellin' yuh about, from Oregon, or up thataway. Funny, ain't it? Talkin' about him today, and got him on our hands tonight — dead."

Big Medicine came in and sat down. His face was very grave, as he rested his big hands on his knees and squinted thoughtfully. Ike handed him the knife and he hefted it in his hand.

"I don't think that Blair ever threw it," he said. "It looks like one that Pete Torres might use."

"If Blair had nothin' to do with it, why did he start shootin' at Stevens?" asked Musical.

"I don't know, Musical."

Big Medicine handed back the knife.

"This will start trouble, won't it?" asked Hashknife.

"Very likely," said Big Medicine. "The K-10 outfit is not a crew of men you can talk things over with."

"I'll tell yuh what we'll do," suggested Hashknife. "We'll pack the body in close to Pinnacle and swear that we met him and he started shootin'. That'll let you folks out of it."

"That's it," agreed Sleepy. "They'll believe us."

But Big Medicine shook his head quickly. "Since when did the Tumbling H shift a responsibility to a guest?" he demanded. "If Baldy Kern wants battle, he'll get it."

"Suits me," said Musical joyfully. "I've been kinda —"

"Just a moment," begged Hashknife. "We're not askin' to take any responsibility off the Tumblin' H Ranch. There's somethin' wrong about this whole thing, folks. If Torres threw that knife, what did Blair have to do with it? Torres ain't connected with the K-10, is he?"

"No, he sure ain't," declared Ike.

"Find Blair's horse," said Hashknife. "He didn't walk here."

Musical, Cleve, Ike, and Sleepy went horse-hunting, while Big Medicine watched Lucy draw most of the swelling from Hashknife's injury. The hilt of the knife had bruised the scalp a little, but it would not be noticeable after the swelling was out.

"Torres probably threw that knife, saw you fall, and headed for the border," said Big Medicine. "It isn't often that he misses. Possibly he hurried his throw and misjudged the distance in the dark."

"Always somethin' to be thankful for," grinned Hashknife. "It always seems that things might 'a' been worse."

In a few minutes the boys came in. They had found Blair's gray horse, branded with the K-10, and brought it up to the house.

"What's the next thing to do?" asked Ike.

"We'll put Blair on his horse and take him to town," said Hashknife. "Me and Sleepy found him beside the road when we were comin' in from this ranch, and we don't know a thing about how he got killed. There's somethin' wrong, and if we make a mystery about this, mebbe somebody will show their cards."

Big Medicine nodded gravely.

"Possibly. I wish we could settle this without open warfare, but I do not want you to take the blame. Blair had no right to be here tonight. He knew that I had drawn a deadline against the K-10, and he knew that I would keep my word."

They loaded Blair's body on his horse, roped it on with Blair's rope, and saddled their own horses. Hashknife walked with only a slight limp and was able to mount his horse without much suffering. His head ached slightly, but otherwise he felt able to take care of himself.

"Come out tomorrow mornin'," invited Big Medicine.

"Come tonight," said Lucy. "We got plenty bed."

"Thank yuh," grinned Hashknife. "We'll see how this deal will work out. So long."

CHAPTER
SIX

KNIFE OR GUN?

They rode away from the ranch over the road which led to Pinnacle, while the lights from the open door of the Tumbling H faded in the distance.

"So Sam Blair was the puncher from Oregon, eh?" said Hashknife.

"Kinda looks like it," agreed Sleepy. "He had that lantern up close to his head and I knowed him right away. I'll betcha he recognized you, Hashknife."

"He sure would."

Hashknife squinted ahead, as he visualized the day that he and Sleepy had busted up a little gang in the Idaho hills, a gang of four horse-thieves. Sam Blair had been the sole survivor. They turned him over to the sheriff, and he had later wounded a deputy sheriff and made his escape.

"Mebbe it's a good thing he's passed on," observed Hashknife. "Blair could do us a lot of harm, if he's connected with a bad outfit down here. We'll just set tight and see which way things jump. Either Blair tried to kill me with a knife, or he was connected with Torres. I don't think Blair done it. He got a good look at me, and when you showed up he got panicky and started throwin' lead. But what was he there for?"

"Don't ask me," replied Sleepy. "I ain't no use when it comes to thinkin' things out. Where did we find Blair?"

"Right here."

The road turned sharply around the point of a hill with brush on each side. Hashknife dismounted and kicked around in the brush, digging his heels into the dirt and otherwise making it appear as though the body had been found there. Sleepy forced the horses to turn several times in the road.

Then, as sort of an afterthought, Hashknife drew the long knife from inside his shirt bosom and tossed it near the spot.

"Somebody'll recognize that knife, Sleepy," he said as he mounted. "We'll give 'em somethin' to quarrel about."

They rode into town and up to the front of the Greenback Saloon, where they dismounted and tied their horses. Lon Pelly was in a poker game, sitting across the table from Baldy Kern. Cloudy Day leaned against the bar, talking with two of the men from the K-10. The other games were fairly well patronized, and the two-piece orchestra was dispensing music to three couples of dancers. Hashknife went to the poker game and spoke directly to Lon Pelly.

"You better step out here a minute, Sheriff," he said. "I've got a dead man."

"You've got a what?" blurted the sheriff, half-rising.

"Dead man," repeated Hashknife. "Found him beside the road between here and the Tumbling H."

"F'r gosh' sakes!"

Lon Pelly upset his pile of poker chips in getting to his feet. The table was deserted in a moment, as all the players wanted to see who the corpse might be. They filed outside and helped Sleepy untie the body and take it into the saloon.

Baldy Kern swore softly as he looked at Blair's body. There was little doubt in his mind that Torres or Garcia had killed Blair.

"Where did yuh find him?" asked the sheriff.

"About a mile from here, out toward the Tumblin' H," said Hashknife. "He was lyin' near the road, and his horse had kinda got tangled in the brush. Do yuh know who he is?"

"Sam Blair," said Baldy. "Worked for me."

The crowd ringed the body, while the sheriff made his examination.

"Knife or gun?" queried Baldy.

"Gun — twice," said the sheriff. "Good shootin'."

He opened the dead man's shirt and covered the two wounds with the palm of his hand.

"Wasn't no nervous finger on that trigger, gents. Sam Blair never knowed what hit him."

"Didja find his gun?" asked Baldly, examining the empty holster.

"Never looked," replied Hashknife. " Probably there in the dirt."

"We'll take a look in the mornin'," said the sheriff. "Some of you boys take the body down to the doctor's place, will yuh? I'm right in a big jackpot. Anyway, there ain't nothin' I can do."

Several of the men carried Blair's body down to the doctor's house, so Hashknife and Sleepy went along.

The doctor was properly indignant, and told them in plain language that he was not running a morgue, so they trooped back uptown with the body.

The doctor recognized Hashknife and Sleepy as being two of the men who had brought in the wounded stranger, and spoke to them about him, asking if they knew where he could get a nurse.

"You might get Mrs. Hawkworth," said Hashknife. "She sure is a good nurse."

"The Indian woman? Hm-m-m. I wonder if she would take the case. This man is out of danger, but needs a nurse badly. I can't be here all the time, and I hate to leave him to the mercies of some man who knows nothing about nursing."

"How long before he'll be able to navigate?" asked Hashknife.

"Two weeks at least."

"Well, I dunno about the Indian woman," said Hashknife. "I'll ask her."

"You'd be doing me a big favor," said the doctor. "I've got to get someone pretty soon."

They went back to the Greenback and found that the body had been deposited in a vacant storeroom for the present. There was much speculation over who killed Blair, but Baldy Kern said nothing. He felt sure that Torres and Garcia had killed him. Jack Baum, who had been Blair's bunkie, knew that Blair had ridden out to

69

see where Torres went, and he also believed that Torres or Garcia had killed him.

The sheriff was too interested in the poker game to speculate on who might have killed Blair. Hashknife and Sleepy stood at the bar, listening to the buzz of conversation.

Lee Yung, the big Chinaman, was at the bar, sipping a drink, his inscrutable eyes taking in the activity of the place.

A little later the sheriff dropped out of the game and came to the bar. He had fared badly, and was not in good humor.

"Got three full-houses beat, hand-runnin'," he complained. "When they do that to yuh, it's time to quit."

"Before that, if possible," said Lee Yung in perfect English.

"That's right," laughed the sheriff. "Saves money, if you've got sense enough to see it."

The stage line owner came into the saloon, saw the sheriff and came to him.

"I just got word from Caliente," he complained hurriedly. "They couldn't tell just how much of a haul the robbers got off the stage, but there was a valuable package for Hawkworth in the treasure box. I think Hawkworth's package was valued at five hundred dollars."

"For Big Medicine, eh?" mused the sheriff.

Hashknife and Sleepy had heard what was said, as had Lee Yung. The sheriff turned to Hashknife.

"When will you see Hawkworth again?" he asked.

70

"Tomorrow mornin', I reckon."

"All right. You tell him about that package, will yuh?"

"Sure thing."

The agent went out and the sheriff went hunting for another chance to lose his money. He was an inveterate gambler. Lee Yung finished his drink and crossed to the roulette game, while Hashknife and Sleepy went to the hotel, engaged a room, and put their horses in the hotel stable.

"Well," said Sleepy, "we got away with it, cowboy. They never even questioned us closely."

"That's true," agreed Hashknife. "I wish I knew who Kern suspects. He kept his mouth shut tight, 'cause he thinks he's got the deadwood on somebody. And there was a valuable package on that stage for Big Medicine, valued at five hundred dollars."

"We're here to cure yore rheumatism," reminded Sleepy.

"I'm cured," grinned Hashknife.

"Then we might as well roll our little ball of yarn out of here, eh?"

Hashknife squinted thoughtfully at the little oil lamp in their room, as he painfully bent his knee in removing a boot.

"Well," he said slowly, "I ain't exactly cured, Sleepy, but I'm recoverin'. That hot water sure is great medicine."

"Between that and a pretty girl to bring yuh hot whiskey."

Hashknife grinned widely.

"Y'betcha. I'd hate to be cured too quick. I noticed her smilin' at you, Sleepy."

"Yuh did not," indignantly.

"I did too. I asked her if she liked you and she says, '*Kiwa teahwit.*'"

"What does that mean?"

"I dunno," said Hashknife innocently. "There's a lot of that language I don't *sabe* myself. Anyway she smiled at yuh, so it must be all right."

"I s'pose," agreed Sleepy. "They're real nice folks at that ranch."

He walked to the window of their room, which was on the ground floor, and looked out. The night stage was just leaving, after waiting for the delayed mail from the Greenhorn Mines, and in the light from the hotel office, Sleepy was able to get a fairly clear view of the equipage.

He watched it disappear and turned to Hashknife, who was already in bed.

"The stage just left, and that big Chinaman was on the seat with the driver," he said.

Hashknife rubbed his nose on the edge of the blanket and grinned at Sleepy.

"Didja want him for anythin'?"

"Not that anybody knows about," retorted Sleepy. "I jist said that he went away on the stage. If you'd 'a' told me that, I'd be supposed to marvel to beat hell and lose sleep over it, wouldn't I?"

Hashknife nodded thoughtfully.

"Thank yuh, Mr. Stevens. I sure do appreciate your information. C'mon to bed, you limber-jawed saddle-slicker. Just because yuh saved my life tonight don't give yuh no license to get sarcastic with me."

72

"I never saved yore life," declared Sleepy. "Sam Blair wasn't tryin' to kill yuh. He was jist lookin' at yuh. I saved my own life, if anybody rises up to inquire."

"Well, don't brag about it, Sleepy. If yuh ever do anythin' real big, I'd like to hear about it, but don't bother me with little incidents. Blow out that lamp, if yuh ain't run out of wind, and c'mon to bed."

Early the following morning Ike Marsh rode into Pinnacle. He was too anxious to wait for the news, so came in to get it first hand. Guarded inquiries revealed the fact that Hashknife and Sleepy were at the hotel, and a short conversation with one of the swampers at the Greenback Saloon informed him that the body of Sam Blair was in a vacant storeroom.

Then Baldy Kern and Jack Baum rode in and tied their horses at the Greenback rack. Ike, being discreet, went out the back door and came around to the front just in time to meet the sheriff.

"Howdy, Lon," he said, wondering just how much the sheriff knew.

"Hello, Ike," returned the sheriff. "What do yuh know?"

Ike shook his head. That was the trouble; he wanted to know something. The sheriff squinted at the horses at the rack.

"Baldy Kern rode in early," he observed. "I reckon he wants to see where Sam Blair was shot. Yuh heard about it, didn't yuh?"

Ike spat dryly and shook his head. The sheriff told him about Hashknife and Sleepy's finding Blair's body beside the road, and Ike marveled greatly.

"Who done it, do yuh suppose?" he asked.

"Gosh only knows, Ike. Somebody sure shot straight. Here comes Hartley and his pardner."

Hashknife and Sleepy were coming from the hotel, heading for the restaurant. Ike and the sheriff met them just as Baldy and Baum came from the saloon. Baldy scowled at Ike and got one in return, while Hashknife shook hands all around.

"I'd kinda like to see where yuh found Sam Blair," said Baldy.

"Right away," agreed Hashknife. "Me and Sleepy was goin' to start for the Tumblin' H, so, we'll all ride out to the spot."

It did not take them long to ride to where Hashknife and Sleepy had planted the signs of conflict, and Baldy was the one to find the knife. He looked it over carefully, and handed it to the sheriff.

"Some toad-sticker," admitted the sheriff, testing the point with his thumb, as he scrutinized the ground carefully.

Baldy and Jack Baum exchanged knowing glances. That Torres had killed Sam Blair was a certainty now. They had seen Torres with that knife.

But search as they might, they could not find Blair's gun.

"Hell, the murderer took it," declared Baum. "He lost his knife, but took the gun. We'll get him, y'betcha."

Satisfied that they could find nothing more, Baldy, Baum, and the sheriff rode back toward town, while Hashknife, Sleepy, and Ike went on to the Tumbling H, where Big Medicine sat on the rickety porch and waited for the news.

Ike told him the whole story before Hashknife had a chance to explain anything.

"They even threw that knife away where Baldy could find it," declared Ike. "By golly, they sure drawed the wool over Lon Pelly's eyes, too. I seen Baldy look at Jack Baum when Baldy found that knife, and I'll betcha they *know* who killed Blair."

Big Medicine nodded approvingly.

"Thank you, boys. It will save a lot of trouble. Come in and eat breakfast."

"That's right," grinned Sleepy. "We didn't take time to eat in town."

Big Medicine explained things to Lucy and Wanna, and the old squaw grinned delightedly, as she examined Hashknife's wound of the night before.

"All gone," she declared.

"Yo're some doctor," smiled Hashknife, patting her on the shoulder.

He turned to Big Medicine, who was sitting down at the table.

"Hawkworth, I had a talk with the doctor last night about that young feller who got shot the night we came in. The doctor can't get anybody to nurse this feller, to look after him while the doctor is out on his cases.

"He's kinda up against it, don'tcha know it. I suggested that he get yore wife to nurse this sick man. She sure could do a good job of it, and I feel sorry for the doc."

75

Big Medicine stared at Hashknife and looked at Lucy.

"No," he said gruffly. "Lucy don't need a job."

"It ain't that," assured Hashknife. "The doc knows that she don't need the money."

But Big Medicine shook his head.

"No, I need her here, Hartley."

"Well, all right," said Hashknife. "I just mentioned it."

Big Medicine said little during the meal. He seemed doubly thoughtful, and his eyes were often turned toward Hashknife, as if wondering why Hashknife should concern himself with this stranger.

From the living-room came the squeaky strains of "The Holy City." Musical Matthews, the last to arise, was having his "morning's morning," as usual. No one commented on it, as they were all used to it by this time.

Sleepy looked up from his breakfast and caught Wanna's eye. She smiled at him and he dropped an egg off his knife onto his lap. Hashknife saw the egg fall and gave Sleepy a reproachful look. Wanna giggled and turned back to the stove.

"Mrs. Hawksworth, if you've got a rough knife, I wish you'd give it to Sleepy," said Hashknife. "The one he's got is too slick."

"I look," said Lucy seriously, and Ike went into a paroxysm of mirth.

He had seen Sleepy trying to rescue the egg, which managed to elude him. Wanna entered into the spirit of the thing and presented Sleepy with a pancake-turner.

76

Sleepy thanked her, upset his coffee with a careless elbow, and withdrew from the room, thankful to escape. Big Medicine looked reprovingly at Wanna, but did not know exactly what it was about, while Lucy still searched for a rough-bladed knife.

After breakfast Big Medicine drew Hashknife aside. They walked down by the corral and stopped in the shade of the stable.

"I heard last night that there was a package valued at five hundred dollars and consigned to you on that stage the other night," said Hashknife. "It was among the stolen stuff, according to the manager of the stage office at Pinnacle."

If Hashknife expected Big Medicine to show surprise, he was disappointed. The big man seemed not at all interested in the news.

"I was just wondering," he said slowly, "why you suggested that my wife act as nurse for Doctor Henry."

"Well, I dunno," said Hashknife. "Mebbe it was 'cause she was the only woman I knew in this country, and because, she knows how to take care of folks."

"I see." Big Medicine nodded slowly. "I'm sorry, but such a thing is impossible, Hartley. I couldn't get along without her."

"How about bringin' the sick man out here?"

"No, I couldn't think of such a thing."

Hashknife squatted on his heels and began rolling a cigarette. Ike and Cleve came down past them, going to the stable, and Big Medicine told them to take things easy until he decided what he wanted them to do today.

"Hawkworth," said Hashknife, after, the boys had gone, "there's somethin' wrong around this country."

Big Medicine looked at Hashknife, but did not reply.

"You lost five hundred dollars in that holdup," continued Hashknife, "and a man was shot without visible cause. Last night someone tried to kill me with a knife. Sleepy killed a man who was lookin' me over, and his own friends didn't ask many questions. What's it all about?"

Big Medicine leaned back against the barn and looked off across the hills.

"I don't know," he said softly. "Maybe there is something wrong." He turned to Hashknife. "Are you a detective?"

Hashknife smiled and shook his head.

"Not guilty, Hawkworth."

"Then why are you interested?"

"Curiosity, I reckon. And you've got to figure that I was in that holdup, and that I got hit last night. Ain't that enough to make me interested?"

"Yes, I suppose so."

"All right. Will yuh do me a big favor, Hawkworth?"

"I don't know."

"Have 'em bring that stranger out here to the ranch. It'll only be a matter of two weeks at the most."

Big Medicine frowned heavily.

"Just why do you want him here, Hartley?"

"I just want to play my hunch. Do you know what a hunch is?"

"Yes. But where does he come in?"

"They shot him, Hawkworth. He had his hands in the air when they shot him."

"M-m-m. You think he knows —"

"Holdup men don't make a practice of shootin' strangers."

"No, I suppose not. But will you be able to find out anything from him?"

"I'm not goin' to ask him questions. As far as he's concerned, he'll be just a sick man. What do yuh say?"

Big Medicine thought it over for a full minute. Then:

"I'll have Ike and Cleve hitch up the wagon team, Hartley. I think Lucy can fix up a room for him."

Big Medicine went striding over to the house, while Hashknife grinned and rolled a cigarette.

Musical Matthews was busy at the phonograph, so Sleepy left him and went to the kitchen door, where Wanna and Lucy were washing the breakfast dishes. Big Medicine came in and stopped near the middle of the room.

"I'm goin' to send Ike and Cleve to Pinnacle with the wagon," he told Lucy. "They'll bring that young feller out here to stay awhile, the one that got shot. Can you take care of him?"

Lucy thought it over for a moment.

"I fix room," she said simply, and turned back to her work.

Big Medicine walked past Sleepy and went into the living-room. Wanna went outside, carrying some chicken feed, and Sleepy stepped into the kitchen.

"I just wanted to ask yuh a question," he told Lucy softly. "What does 'kiwa teahwit' mean?"

"*Kiwa teahwit?*" repeated Lucy thoughtfully. "I forget some word. Mm-m-m." She looked up and smiled. "That mean crooked leg. Jus' like how leg, I think."

Sleepy flushed slightly and his lips compressed a trifle.

"Does Wanna *sabe* that language?" he asked.

Lucy shook her head. "Wanna never hear. Long times I no hear."

"Thank yuh," nodded Sleepy, and went outside.

Ike and Cleve were hitching a team to the wagon. Big Medicine and Musical came out of the front door and walked down where Hashknife squatted in the shade of the stable.

Ike and Cleve drove away, and Sleepy went down to join those at the stable.

"What do yuh know about Lee Yung the Chinaman?" asked Hashknife.

"Not much," replied Musical. "He's a plunger, I *sabe* that much. Yuh can't tell anythin' about a Chink, but I'd bet my last cent that Lee Yung is a smuggler. I tell yuh there's Chinks bein' run through this country, and drugs. Lee Yung ain't the kind that would waste his time over what he can win in Pinnacle."

"He went out on the stage last night," offered Sleepy.

"Thasso? Well, if I was a officer I'd watch that Chink."

"Talks good English," said Hashknife.

"And thinks like an Oriental, I suppose," smiled Big Medicine. "It is a dangerous combination. I have never met Lee Yung. I feel morally responsible for Hawk

Hole, and I hope that Musical is wrong about the drug-smuggling. As far as the smuggling of Chinese is concerned, I have nothing to say.

"They are not a menace as far as I can understand. Our Government admits many emigrants less desirable than Chinese. Except in rare cases, the Chinese are a peaceable race, and their troubles are only their own people. Unlike the whites, they are a bit particular whom they kill."

"That's right," grinned Hashknife. "They seem to draw the color line. I've never seen one that would lie. They either tell yuh the truth, or tell yuh nothin'."

"I wish more white men were thataway," said Sleepy, looking seriously at Hashknife. "A lot of fellers' brains and tongues are *kiwa teahwit*."

Hashknife squinted closely at Sleepy, and his face broke into a wide grin. Big Medicine was not looking at either of them.

"Lucy got a lot of pleasure out of exchanging a few words in the trade language with you," he said. "She said it was like seeing some of her own people again. None of the rest of us ever understood the language."

"That's what I understand," said Sleepy, and Hashknife smothered a laugh in the sleeve of his shirt.

The joke had gone over better than he had anticipated.

CHAPTER
SEVEN

THE MAN WITH THE WAXED MUSTACHE

It was about a week later, well past midnight, when the stage rattled down the grades which led into Hawk Hole. Olsen, the regular driver, was alone on the seat, with one passenger inside the stage.

They swept into the Hole and out onto the flat country, the four horses running at top speed. Far ahead of them a lantern blinked beside the road. Olsen drew the team down to a trot and stopped near the lantern, where a man held the heads of a team hitched to a buckboard.

The man climbed down from inside the stage and walked over to the lantern. He was a big man, almost as big as Big Medicine Hawkworth, and of about the same age. But this man's face was pale and heavily lined, with a hawklike nose and piercing black eyes. His white mustache was waxed to needlelike points, and his white hair curled down around his shoulders from beneath a wide-brimmed, black hat.

"Well, yuh got here, Doc," observed Baldy Kern, who held the team. "I just got here myself."

"That wild devil of a driver swore he'd get me here on time," replied the big man. "My God, I almost prayed several times."

Olsen laughed loudly, whirled his long whip over the team, and rattled away in a cloud of dust. Baldy and the big man got into the buckboard, swung the team around, and headed across country toward the K-10 Ranch.

"Lee Yung didn't come with yuh, eh?" queried Baldy, when he had slowed up to circle a washout.

"He came through last night. I thought it would be best. What is the latest news?"

"I don't know any news," replied Baldy. "Yuh see, I dunno what it's all about. Lee Yung didn't know either, Doc. We thought somethin' was wrong, so Lee tells me he's goin' to Frisco and see Doc Meline. I ain't seen Lee since he came back."

"You didn't get my letter, eh?" asked Doctor Meline.

"I dunno anythin' about a letter."

"The letter I sent you a few days before somebody held up the stage."

"I didn't git no letter from yuh, Doc."

For some distance Doctor Meline remained silent. Then:

"Kern, I am only asking for a square deal. If you and the gang thought you could get that twenty thousand dollars —"

"Hold on!"

Kern jerked the horses to a stop and turned angrily to the big man.

"None of that, Doc. If you sent twenty thousand dollars by that stage, we never seen any of it."

"I beg your pardon," said Meline quickly. "I just wanted to know, Kern."

"Well, you found out. Git up!"

They drove on in silence for another mile. Then —

"Mind explainin' a few things?" asked Baldy.

"I came here to explain and to listen to explanations. I sent that twenty thousand dollars to Hawkworth, and I wrote you a letter, previous to shipping it, telling you when it would come. Who got that letter?"

"I didn't," said Baldy shortly,

"Who takes your mail out to the ranch from Pinnacle?"

"Anybody who happens to be in town."

"Then there's a traitor at the K-10, Kern."

"You think that one of my men opened the letter?"

"And got help to rob that stage — yes."

"You're wrong, Doc. The night that stage was robbed every one of my men were at the ranch. Not a damn one of 'em was away."

"And the man who was shot that night, Kern. How is he?"

"All right, I reckon. Yuh see, they took him out to Hawkworth's ranch."

"To Hawkworth's ranch! Is that where he is now?"

"Well, I reckon he is, Doc. Doctor Henry couldn't get a nurse to take care of him, so they shipped him out there. I suppose he's gettin' along all right."

"Well, I'll be damned!" The big man exploded into a booming laugh.

84

"Who is he?" asked Baldy, after Meline's mirth had subsided.

"Who is he? Kern, that young man is my son — Jack Meline."

"No!"

"Yes."

"Uh-huh." Baldy drew the team to a slow walk. "Doc, did you send him in here to spy on us?"

"Spy on you?"

"Yeah, spy on us. Now listen to me, Doc. If you don't think that we're givin' you a square deal, hire somebody else. Don't spy. We've got to trust each other, or go bust. We're both crooks, but we can't afford to be crooked with each other. I'll run this end of the game and you run your end."

"Fair enough, Kern, but remember this: I can get men to run your end of it, but you can't replace me."

"That won't keep me from quittin'," replied Kern softly. "If I've got to watch you and watch some other gang who are tryin' to bust up our game, I'll quit. One of my men was killed the night that Lee Yung left for Frisco."

"The Chinaman told me. His name was Blair, if I remember correctly."

"Yeah, it was Blair, I sent him out to trail Torres."

"And Torres killed him, did he? Why didn't you kill Torres?"

"Down in this country," said Baldy slowly, "yuh most always have to find a man before yuh can kill him."

"Where is he?"

"I dunno. Mebbe he's down at the Rancho Sierra."

"Why not hire Steve Guadalupe to kill him?"

"That's a fine idea. They're both Mexicans, and Steve is making too much easy money to be attracted by blood money."

They drove up to the K-10, and Baldy turned the team over to Jack Baum.

The K-10 ranch-house was a long adobe structure, situated on the edge of a mesa, which gave a fairly good view of the sweeping expanse of Hawk Hole. About a third of the house was used as a kitchen and dining-room, while the other two thirds was a combination living-quarters and bunkhouse.

Behind the house was a long series of low sheds and several corrals. Baldy introduced Doctor Meline to all the boys, except the Mexican cook, José, whose English was limited to profanity.

"I've seen you before, Doc," said "Two Fingers" Kohler, a hard-faced cowpuncher, who had lost three fingers from his left hand in an argument with a Mexican.

"Have you?" smiled the big man.

"Yeah, in Frisco," nodded Kohler. "You was standin' on a platform, under one of them gas'line lights, sellin' some kind of damned remedy. Yo're kinda slick with cards, ain'tcha? By golly, yuh shore done some cute tricks, but I don't s'pose that medicine would cure anythin'."

Meline flushed slightly and lighted a cigar. He had been the prince of faker doctors until the police had stopped him from peddling a quack nostrum, a guaranteed cure-all, which was probably made from colored water and quinine.

The newspapers had taken up the case, and the resultant advertising had caused Doctor Meline to return to his big home out near the Presidio, where he proceeded to forget that he ever hawked cheap medicine with a ballyhoo, and to engage in a business of big returns with less publicity.

"Did yuh hear anythin' from the Tumblin' H today, Jack?" asked Baldy.

"Not a thing," replied Baum. "I seen Hartley and Stevens in town, but they was only there a few minutes."

"Who are they?" asked Meline curiously.

"Couple of punchers," said Baldy. "One of 'em had rheumatism and come here to bathe in Hawkworth's hot water."

"Yes?" Meline smoked slowly, thoughtfully. "Came here to bathe, in the hot springs, eh? How long have they been here?"

"They came the night of the holdup."

"Did they? Hm-m-m. The night of the holdup. And what have they done since?"

"One of 'em stood Torres on his head in the blacksmith's slack tub," grinned Baldy. "They were the ones who found Blair after he was killed."

"Yeah," said Kohler, "and I heard Doctor Henry say that Hartley was the one who got Hawkworth to take that wounded man out to the Tumblin' H Ranch."

"Well!" Meline removed his cigar and grinned at Baldy. "It seems that these two cowpunchers have been real active. Baldy, did it ever occur to you that a stranger might be dangerous?"

"You mean, they might be —"

Baldy hesitated. Meline's smile was sneering, pitying.

"You poor fool, of course! Did you think that the Government would hire flat-footed detectives to investigate in a cattle country?"

Baldy flushed angrily and got to his feet.

"You cut out that 'fool' stuff, Meline," he warned. "You think that nobody has any brains but you, don'tcha?"

"Don't get riled," advised Meline coldly. "I've got a right to criticize when my life and liberty are concerned."

"Your life and liberty be damned! You're nothin' but a retailer, Meline. We're the ones to take the chances. When bullets start flyin' in Hawk Hole, there's damn few of 'em that'll reach you in Frisco. You've covered yourself pretty damn well. Lee Yung and me are the only ones, until now, that knew who you were."

"All right. We won't argue, Kern. I'm sorry I had to come here. But maybe it is a good thing I did. Perhaps I was hasty in my criticism. I have learned to mistrust everyone."

"You better git that out of yore system," advised Baldy. "I suppose you'll go over to see Hawkworth tomorrow, eh!"

"Don't be a fool, Kern. Hawkworth must not see me, and neither must he know I am here. He is probably the biggest fool I ever knew — but a dangerous fool."

"How long are yuh goin' to stay here?" asked Baldy.

"*Quien sabe?* There are a few things to clear up, Kern. I want to find out who stole that money and shot my son."

"You'll prob'ly be here a hell of a long time. Let's turn in. Take Blair's bunk, if yuh want to. He died in a good cause."

"Thanks. I am not afraid of dead men. They are harmless."

It was the following day at the Tumbling H Ranch that the wounded man came slowly out through the kitchen door and sat down in a blanket-covered rocking chair which had been placed in the shade for him by Lucy.

He was still a trifle shaky, colorless, but able to get around. His thin face twisted wearily as he sat down and brushed back his black hair with a nervous gesture. It was washday at the Tumbling H, and the invalid watched Wanna as she hung out the clothes, her arms bare to the shoulder, her black hair hanging down her back in a big braid.

From around the corner came the everlasting *rub-rub-rub* as Lucy scrubbed the clothes. Down at the corral, Hashknife, Sleepy, and Musical were saddle breaking a colt, and having a big time out of it. The pseudo Jack Hill scowled at them as he rolled a cigarette.

Wanna came back to the corner, carrying the empty basket. Jack smiled up at her and indicated for her to sit down on the steps. But Wanna shook her head with a smile.

"Work to be done," she said.

"I don't know how you stand it to live here all the time," he said. "My God, I'd get the willies sure. And you say you've never been out of here, out of Hawk Hole?"

Wanna turned and scanned the hills, as she shook her head.

"No, I live here all the time."

"That's too bad, Wanna. I feel sorry for yuh. A pretty girl like you in a place like this. You ought to get out and see things, instead of living here and seeing nothing."

"What would I see?" she asked innocently.

"What? My gosh! The world — the cities — everything."

"Everything," she repeated slowly. "What is a city — like Pinnacle?"

Jack laughed at her ignorance. Neither of them knew that Big Medicine had come to the kichen door.

"Not hardly like Pinnacle," said Jack, laughing. "There are many big buildings, many people, bright lights, and — life. You don't *live* out here, Wanna."

"You go back?" she asked.

"You bet. Just as soon as I can travel, I'm going back."

"Maybe I go some day," said Wanna wistfully. "I like to see everything."

"You'd enjoy it. I'd like to show you the city, Wanna."

"You like to show me?" eagerly.

Jack looked sidewise and a crooked smile twisted his lips.

"Yes, I would. You're pretty enough to show to anybody."

Lucy called sharply to Wanna and the girl went reluctantly back to her work. Big Medicine came slowly outside and stopped beside Jack's chair.

"I heard what you said to her."

Big Medicine's voice was pitched low. Jack twisted nervously. He was afraid of this big man.

"Well, what of it?" he asked.

"I've watched you and her," said Big Medicine softly. "Youth calls to youth, they say; but not in this case. I know your type, Jack Hill. The honor of a pretty girl means nothing to you. The cities are filled with young men like you, idlers, wine hounds — and worse.

"Wanna is a half-breed. Her Indian blood makes her believe what you tell her, while her white blood makes a romance of your mysterious shooting. You are something new to her. You do not talk the language of the hills and cattle ranges, and she puts you above the rest of the men.

"You are trying to make her unhappy with her life, with your word pictures of the cities. You wouldn't marry her. To you she is a pretty girl, ignorant as a savage, something to play with. Let me tell you something, Jack Hill," Big Medicine leaned closer and lowered his voice to a whisper. "If you harm her in any way, by words or by actions, I'll kill you. That is my promise."

Big Medicine turned away and went back into the house, while Jack humped in his chair, his lips shut tightly, while the cigarette between his fingers, still glowing, was crushed to powder.

Inwardly he cursed Big Medicine, but deep in his heart he knew that Big Medicine spoke the truth. And he knew that the big man would keep his promise. But he hated Big Medicine now. It was true that he had filled Wanna's ears with tales of faraway places, many of them untrue, but today was the first time that she had intimated that she would care to see these places.

From inside his shirt he drew out a little silk-covered parcel, hardly larger than an ordinary pocketbook. He seemed careful that no one might see what he was doing. Twisting the thing in his right hand, he opened a flexible corner and poured a tiny bit of the white powder on his left wrist.

He lifted his left hand toward his face, an innocent enough motion, brought the tiny bit of powder in contact with his nostrils — a sniff — and it was gone. The silken bag was put back inside his shirt. Thereupon Jack Hill shrugged his shoulders, sighed deeply, contentedly, and became at peace with the world.

Just one person saw what he had done — Big Medicine. He had stood at the kitchen window, wondering what effect his warning would have, and he had seen Jack Hill take his dose of cocaine. Big Medicine turned away, shaking his head, but resolving to be rid of Jack Hill as soon as possible. Hashknife came up from the corral and stopped for a moment to chat with Jack.

"Feelin' better, eh?" he commented. "Yore color is better today. This is sure a great place to get well, pardner. It cured me of rheumatism in a week."

"I feel pretty good," replied Jack, none too graciously. "I'm all fed up on this place, though, and the sooner I get out the better it will suit me."

"Yeah? Well, that's too bad, Hill. They've been mighty good to yuh here. Mrs. Hawkworth sure done a lot for you."

"She'll be well paid for it," gruffly.

"Yeah, I s'pose," Hashknife sighed. "She done a lot for me too, but I won't be able to pay much. Still, I can sure be just as grateful as I can be to her and Wanna."

"You rather like Wanna too, don't you?" There was a sneer in Jack's voice.

"Rather," said Hashknife softly.

"I thought so. Well, don't let me stand in your way, Hartley."

Hashknife's eyes half-closed as he looked at the younger man, a look that other men had seen just before a swift draw.

"Hill," he said icily, "yo're walkin' a narrow trail. Wanna is a mighty-sweet girl, and I'm old enough to be her father. Yo're not in my way, young feller. If you was, I'd tie you in a hard knot, so damned hard that nothin' would ever untie yuh. Personally, I don't think yo're worth the dynamite it would take to blow yuh to hell. Now yuh know where I stand."

"I'm going to worry a lot about that," sneered Hill.

He was stimulated to a point where nothing would make him realize his foolishness. His eyes were slightly glassy and he laughed immoderately. Hashknife looked at him curiously, turned, and went into the kitchen.

CHAPTER
EIGHT

QUITE A LOT OF NEWS

Ike Marsh rode in from Pinnacle and turned his horse into the corral. Ike had suffered another session of poker, which was one of his chief vices, but this time the Greenback Saloon took most of his previous winnings.

He came up to the house, where he found Hashknife and Big Medicine in the living-room. "Wasn't no mail," he told Big Medicine. "Torres and Garcia came to Pinnacle last night, and Lee Yung came in on the stage yesterday mornin'. And that's all the news."

"That's quite a lot," observed Hashknife thoughtfully. "I wonder what will happen now, Hawkworth. Both parties have been gone quite a while."

"That's hard to tell. If Baldy Kern thinks that Torres killed Blair, he will probably try to kill Torres. If Torres did try to kill you, and finds that he failed, he will probably try again."

"Sounds reasonable," grinned Hashknife. "I reckon I'll ride to Pinnacle this evenin'. If Mr. Torres wants another chance, I'll sure give it to him, unless Kern beats me to it."

"I'm goin' back," said Ike quickly. "I've got enough left to buy a couple stacks of white chips, and I ain't so sure but what I profited by my lesson of last night. I reckon Musical and Cleve intends to go in tonight."

Ike knew that neither Musical nor Cleve had any idea of going to Pinnacle that night, but he was paving the way for the Tumbling H to be well represented in case of trouble.

"This is not our trouble," Big Medicine reminded him.

"Oh, sure not."

Ike hadn't the slightest idea of mixing into any trouble. He went out, rattling his spurs, as he hurried down to tell Cleve and Musical that they were going to Pinnacle that night.

Hashknife smiled softly at Big Medicine. They had become fast friends during Hashknife's short stay at the Tumbling H.

"The boys are worth having at your back," said Big Medicine.

"Thank yuh," said Hashknife. "It kinda looks like there ain't nothin' in my hunch this time. The bunch from the K-10 seem as friendly as anyone could be to me. Lookin' at it from the outside, all is serene.

"I've wanted to tell yuh for quite a while that me and Sleepy knew Sam Blair up in the Northwest. We rounded him up in a raid on a horse-thief gang, in which Blair was the only survivor. He escaped later, after shootin' a deputy sheriff, and nobody up there knowed where he went.

"I can't quite figure out what he was doin' out here that night. I don't think he knew that we were in this country. It is hardly possible that he recognized Sleepy,

96

but started shootin' because he knowed he was caught."

"I wondered if you didn't know him," said Big Medicine. "Sleepy did not ask questions after the killing, and it seemed to me that he knew the man. But you have a poker face, Hartley. When you heard who had been killed, you did not change expression."

"Mebbe I wasn't quite right in the head," grinned Hashknife. "I got quite a tunk that night. I reckon we'll stick around till the last of the week, and if nothin' happens we'll drift."

"Stay as long as you wish," said Big Medicine quickly. "The Tumbling H is your home, Hartley, and it will be mighty lonesome when you leave. The boys like you and Sleepy, and I know how Lucy and Wanna feel toward both of you. Wanna isn't the kind to say things, but I can tell. And let me tell you something" — Big Medicine smiled broadly — "Lucy says to me, 'We must get more cattle.' I asked her why we should get more cattle, and she said, 'Hire two more cowboys.'"

Hashknife laughed softly over his cigarette.

"Mebbe she likes us because I talk a little of the language she ain't heard for a long time, Hawkworth."

"Perhaps. But she says nothing about that part of it. Lucy likes company. I'm English, Hartley. I was born of a family in which there was too much money and too many sons. I was educated in England, brought up with some queer traditions in my brain, some queer ideas, you might call them.

"You wonder why I married a squaw? God knows, I sometimes wonder why myself. Perhaps it was because

I lost faith. But no matter. Lucy has been a good wife. I suppose I did not realize what I was doing when I married her, but the realization came later."

Big Medicine hooked his hands over his knees and stared at the threadbare carpet, deep in thought.

"The realization," he continued softly, "was the fact that my children would be half-breeds. They could never take their place with the whites. It seemed to me that the Indian blood would predominate, always. And one reason for that would be the fact that they would know that they had an Indian mother.

"You have known Indians and half-breeds, Hartley. And you know that the half-breed never measures up. They inherit the vices of both bloods and the virtues of neither. They are a weak-kneed, and often treacherous combination.

"And that realization hurt, Hartley. I suppose it is the old pride of ancestry cropping out; my inheritance of a hidebound pride, in which the children are the greater. It was like a blow in the face, when the realization came to me. Perhaps I might have left Lucy and married a white woman — but I didn't. I've some of the instincts of a gentleman left, some honor. But I knew that my offspring would always work under the handicap of an Indian mother."

"And knowin' that would make 'em more red than white?" asked Hashknife. "Is that yore theory, Hawkworth?"

"Yes. I wonder" — he lifted his head and looked at Hashknife keenly — "I wonder if a child born of a white man and an Indian woman, brought up away from them and taught to believe that nothing but white blood flowed in his or her veins — would they not be the same as a pure breed?"

"The psychology of ignorance?" smiled Hashknife. "I don't know, Hawkworth. But what satisfaction would that be to either the white man or the Indian squaw? It might be a good experiment, but gosh-awful tough on the parents. By golly, I'd raise my own kid — regardless of who or what its mother might be."

"And not give the child a chance?"

"That's yore hidebound English croppin' out, Hawkworth. If the child was worth a damn, it would make its own chance. Suppose you had done that with Wanna. Would she be any better off?"

"No white man would marry her, Hartley."

"No? Then let her pick a man to suit herself. If a white man won't marry her, what's the odds? You talk like there wasn't any good men in the world except white men. I'm sorry to say that I've done battle with a lot of thieves, crooks, and murderers; many of them are lookin' up at the grass-roots right now — and they were all white men, Hawkworth."

"I get your viewpoint, Hartley. Perhaps you are right. It is only a theory, at best. Living here for twenty-five years, I have had plenty of time for theorizing. It has been a long time, my friend, longer than you can realize. Men say that Big Medicine Hawkworth is a queer person, and that he is unfriendly. Some of them hate me because I own Hawk Hole, and hold it.

"Since the town of Pinnacle was built, Hawk Hole's morals have not improved. The Greenhorn Mines have brought the riffraff of the Southwest into this place, until it seems to be a happy hunting ground for high-graders, cattle-thieves, smugglers. Is it any wonder that I do not welcome a stranger to my home?"

"I figure we were lucky to get in," smiled Hashknife.

Big Medicine's eyes twinkled.

"Do you know what did it? When I asked you what you wanted, you said, 'Not what he got,' referring to Jim Reed, whom I had thrown out of my house. It struck me that your sense of humor was too keen to be owned by less than a gentleman."

Hashknife laughed softly.

"Mr. Reed sure came out. He didn't do any complainin' at all either. Just grabbed his bronc and whaled away from here. I took one look at you, and says to myself, 'Here's the prophet Elijah, wearin' high-heeled boots.'

"And you kinda had a habit of switchin' from good English to cow-town United States, Hawkworth. It was interestin' to me. Some folks had kinda warned us against comin' out to see you; but that would make me come if nothin' else did. If a man or a woman is worth sayin' things against, they're worth meetin'."

"And you've been worth talking to, Hashknife," said Bid Medicine warmly. "I hope your hunch, as you call it, will keep you in Hawk Hole for a long time. My definition of the word 'gentleman' has changed so greatly that I hesitate to use it; so I feel more safe in calling you my friend than a gentleman. I have a bottle of very old whiskey, older than you are, my friend, and I think it is a proper time to drink a health."

"To you," said Hashknife, and Big Medicine went after the bottle.

Pedro Torres was just vain enough over his knife-throwing ability to feel sure that he had killed the man who had humiliated him. Until he came back to Pinnacle there was not a doubt in his mind but that Hashknife Hartley had not lived long enough to know what had struck him.

But discreet questioning had brought him the information that Hashknife Hartley had evidently entirely recovered from his attack of rheumatism and was again enjoying good health.

And it was a distinct shock to hear that Sam Blair had been killed that night halfway between Pinnacle and the Tumbling H Ranch, and that a long-bladed knife had been found at the scene of the killing.

Torres rubbed his chin and considered things. He hated to admit to himself that he had miscalculated his throw, but how did his knife happen to be found near Blair's body? The description of the knife, meager as it was, convinced Torres that it was the one he had flung at Hashknife from the shadows of the bathhouse.

But how had it been found beside a dead man, far removed from the yard of the Tumbling H? Torres rubbed his chin some more and decided that there was some hocus pocus in the wind. He had seen his victim fall. He questioned the slow-witted Garcia.

"He died," declared Garcia in Spanish.

"He lives," retorted Torres. "Sam Blair died a mile or more from the place where I threw the knife, and my knife was found beside him."

"That is evil fortune," said Garcia. "Other men will see that knife and know who owns it."

"Croaking buzzards!" Torres spat angrily. "I must have hurried my throw — and it was dark."

"A mile is a long throw," observed Garcia blandly.

"I will kill you some day for being such a fool," replied Torres. "Still," he reflected, "it was found there, and who would leave it beside the dead body of Sam Blair? He was shot to death."

"Your knife did not kill him?"

"No."

"Then you have nothing to fear."

"If I was not there, how did my knife fall to the ground?" demanded Torres hotly. "Perhaps I shot him and lost the knife."

"Perhaps." Garcia was agreeable. "I think we will be safer across the border."

But Torres shook his head.

"Not yet. Some of these days we might, but not now. There is too much money to be made here."

"A slit throat does not taste wine," said Garcia. "Money is of no value to a corpse. I would rather drink Guadalupe's vile tequila, in safety than to risk my neck for champagne."

"There may be virtue in all that," replied Torres. "Go, if you are afraid. If not, stop croaking. I have business to attend to in Pinnacle. Guadalupe sent a message to Kern yesterday by that half-wit, Perez — who let me read it for the price of a quart of mescal."

"It must have been of great value — to Perez," grinned Garcia.

"We shall later discover its value. Say nothing."

Torres did no more questioning, and was doubly cautious. He felt sure that sooner or later someone would mention the knife to him, and he could not think of a single reason for losing that knife. The only thing he could do would be to deny that he had been near the spot where Blair had died, and swear that he had missed the knife when undressing at the Rancho Sierra.

It was very true that he had missed the knife. It was a favorite blade, and one he had carried a long time. One does not find a good throwing blade every day. He carried a revolver, under his sash and inside the waistband of his trousers; but he was not a gunman, preferring the more silent weapon.

Lee Yung, the fat, bland-faced Chinaman, sat stolidly in a chair at a poker table, pitting his wits against Faro Lanning. The rest of the players were of no moment to Lee Yung, who would bet a thousand dollars with about the same emotion as a sphinx.

Torres wanted to play poker, but not in such fast company, so he confined his efforts to trying to outguess the roulette wheel, where he could also keep an eye on the front door.

It was after dark that Hashknife, Sleepy, Ike Marsh, Musical Matthews, and Cleve Davis came in. They clanked up to the bar and greeted the bartender vociferously. Hashknife saw Torres and grinned widely. Torres tried to smile, but the effort was too great.

In his perturbation he made a foolish bet, and watched the dealer sweep away his money. Hashknife swung away from the bar and came toward the roulette game. He seemed entirely unconcerned, but his eyes took in every move made by the dandy Mexican.

Torres' right hand moved nervously toward his sash, stopped, dropped back to his side. He knew that there was no use of him provoking trouble, so he proceeded to use discretion.

"How's she goin'?" asked Hashknife pleasantly.

"*Buena*," said Torres.

He watched Hashknife place several small bets, wondering why this tall cowpuncher, who had so blithely dumped him into the tub of dirty water, seemed to have forgotten it so soon. He wondered if it was ignorance or bravado.

Hashknife looked up from his bets and studied Torres' clothes.

"You've been away quite a while, ain't yuh, Torres?"

"Did you miss me?"

Torres lifted his eyebrows. Hashknife grinned and shook his head.

"No, I didn't miss yuh, but I see yore clothes are dry."

Torres flushed at the reminder. He did not want to be baited by this man; and yet he did not know how to prevent it, except by walking away. Hashknife was laughing at him, and it suddenly occurred to Torres that this man's laugh was not derisive. The joke seemed to be on Torres, so he laughed with Hashknife.

"That's a lot better," said Hashknife. "There are things that are a lot better to forget, pardner."

104

"I have forgotten them," said Torres earnestly. "Perhaps I made a mistake."

"Mebbe," grinned Hashknife.

Garcia leaned against the wall near the roulette wheel, his arms folded under his dirty serape, feeling of the knife hilt inside his shirt. He heard what Torres said, and his hands came in sight to fumble with a cigarette.

Hashknife drifted away from the wheel and joined Sleepy near the bar.

"I kinda looked for that Mexican to make a break," said Sleepy softly. "I had my eye on that jigger beside the wall, too. He's got somethin' under that dirty blanket thing he's wearin', and I reckon it's a knife. I was just waitin' for somethin' to start and then I was goin' to hang him to the wall on the hot end of a bullet."

"I reckon I've kinda squared things with Torres," observed Hashknife.

"Thasso?" Sleepy scratched his hand on his thigh. "What's the idea of squarin' things with him?"

"I've got to pry into things some way," said Hashknife. "I'm bettin' that there's two outfits in on some kind of a deal, and I've got to dig my way into one of 'em."

"If we showed any sense, we'd dig out of here," reclaimed Sleepy. "Prob'ly get ourselves into a jam over nothin'."

"Somebody got Big Medicine's money, Sleepy."

"Yeah, I know that."

"And somebody tried to kill yore little playmate."

"Well, go ahead, cowboy. I s'pose you could dig up a lot more reasons for stayin' here."

Hashknife laughed. He knew that Sleepy would never quit complaining if they rode out of Hawk Hole without finding out why certain things had happened. It was Sleepy's nature to talk as if he were a prize pessimist.

At about nine o'clock Baldy Kern, Jack Baum, and Two-Fingers Kohler came into the Greenback Saloon. Baldy nodded to Hashknife, as they came up to the bar, and Hashknife and Sleepy moved aside to give them more room.

The three men talked in an undertone, as they drank. It seemed that Baldy cautioned Kohler about something, and Hashknife heard Kohler reply angrily, "Oh, to hell with that Government spy."

Hashknife wondered who Kohler meant, until he saw Jack Baum flash a sidewise look at him, and then he realized that possibly they were talking about him. It was sufficient to put him on his guard.

Baldy turned from the bar and scanned the room. Torres was at the roulette wheel, facing Baldy, but seemingly absorbed in the game. Baldy turned his head slightly toward Baum and spoke guardedly, but too softly for Hashknife to hear what he said.

Then he moved away from the bar, stopped for a moment at the poker table to speak to someone in the game, and sauntered toward the roulette wheel. Baum and Kohler moved away from the bar, keeping their eye on Baldy.

"Look out," whispered Hashknife. "Somethin is due to break."

Baldy was only ten feet from Torres now, and they were looking at each other. The dealer called the winning number, but Torres did not look down at the table.

"You dirty Mexican!" snapped Baldy. "You killed Sam Blair!"

As Baldy spat his accusation he whipped out his gun. Baldy was fast on the draw, as deadly as a striking rattlesnake. But before he could pull the trigger the light flashed on a spinning knife-blade, which Garcia had thrown from beside the wall, and Baldy's wrist was pierced just above the joint.

His hand splayed open and the heavy gun clanged to the floor as he jerked back, throwing up his wounded arm.

Kohler flung himself forward, drawing a gun, but stumbled over Hashknife's outflung foot and lunged heavily to the floor, almost under the roulette wheel. Torres darted toward the front door, while Garcia chose to make his exit at the rear, and all the while Jack Baum was trying to get past the clumsy Sleepy, who seemed to be innocently trying to efface himself from the scene.

It was only a matter of seconds before it was all over. The room was in an uproar. Baldy was swearing painfully, as he tried to check the bleeding of his wrist, assisted by Lee Yung. Kohler was still trying to find his gun, which had flipped out of his hand, and Jack Baum was trying to make up his mind whether Sleepy blocked him intentionally, or whether Sleepy was the most clumsy lout he had ever met.

Kohler's face was scarlet, as he painfully dusted his knees and peered under the roulette wheel, where he found his gun. He holstered it savagely and came back toward the bar. He faced Hashknife, shaking with rage.

"You tripped me!" he snorted. " Damn you, why did you do it?"

"Yore feet are too wide," said Hashknife evenly. "How much room do yuh need?"

The crowd lost interest in Baldy's injuries now.

"You tripped me on purpose!" roared Kohler. "I'll show you how I pay —"

He drew back his right fist and let drive with a blow that was so obvious that Hashknife moved easily aside to avoid it and smashed Kohler square in the center of his wide throat. Kohler seemed to be falling almost before the *splat* of the blow, and he went flat on his face. Hashknife stepped back, his right hand swinging loosely at his side, and glanced around.

Jack Baum was standing almost against the bar, his hands half-raised, while Sleepy was very close to him, his gun-muzzle resting square against Baum's waistline. Baldy's face was gray with pain and anger, but he was in no condition to lend anyone assistance.

Some of the men turned Kohler over on his back, while the bartender poured a glass of water over his face. The knockout was so complete that many of the men ventured the opinion that Kohler was dead. Lee Yung examined him and shook his head.

"He is not badly hurt," was Lee Yung's opinion. "For a long time he will swallow with difficulty, I think."

"Hashknife, you shore pressed his old Adam's apple," applauded Musical Matthews. "My God, what a complete cleanup!"

"You can put down yore hands," said Sleepy to Jack Baum.

Baum lowered his hands, but was careful to keep them away from his gun. Kohler coughed and sat up, painfully massaging his throat, while his eyes squinted around, as if wondering what it was all about. Someone helped him into a chair, and the bartender asked him how he was feeling, but Kohler's voice had fled.

"Tied a knot in his vocal cords," observed Ike gleefully.

Baldy finished bandaging his wrist. Lee Yung found his gun and put it in the holster for Baldy, who came closer to Hashknife.

"I've been wonderin' what you was doin' down here," he said slowly, and loud enough for everyone to hear. "I reckon yo're rheumatism is near enough cured for you to *vamoose*. Take my advice and get out *muy pronto, hombre*.

"Torres killed one of my men, Hartley. You stopped me from payin' him back for this murder, or rather you stopped my men from doin' what I started in to do. Yore breed don't thrive in this country, so take my advice, right now."

Hashknife smiled easily.

"How do you know Torres killed Blair?"

"I know damn well he did!"

"All right. Tell me what Blair was doin' the night Torres is supposed to kill him."

"How in hell do I know!"

"Why would Torres kill him?"

"Well, I — I dunno, but —"

"The fact of the matter is — yo're guessin', Kern. I reckon Blair got what was comin' to him. And as far as Hawk Hole bein' healthy for my breed, I've lived and had my bein' in some damned infested localities. I'll remember what yuh said, Kern. Barkin' dogs don't bite, they say, but they kinda make yuh keep yore head up and yore eyes open."

Baldy squinted at Hashknife and down at his throbbing wrist.

"Mebbe you know who killed Blair," he said.

"Which shows that *you* don't," said Hashknife easily.

Baldy considered the answer for several moments, turned and walked out, followed by Jack Baum. Kohler followed them with his eyes, as if afraid to trust his legs to carry him out. Then he got up from his chair and went unsteadily out into the street.

No one spoke for several moments after they went out. The poker-players went back to their chairs, and the roulette started in where it left off. Faro Lanning came behind the bar to get a drink before renewing his game, and asked Hashknife and Sleepy to partake of his hospitality.

"It ain't none of my business," he said confidentially, "but perhaps you acted right in that matter. Baldy wasn't sure, you see. Personally I don't think that Torres killed Blair. Torres is a knife fighter, pure and

110

simple. Unless it was an accident, Torres could never stick two bullets into any target as close as them two were stuck into Sam Blair. But look out for Kern. Well, here's regards."

They drank to each other and Lanning went back to his game. Lee Yung's expressionless eyes considered Hashknife's back, while they drank at the bar, but turned away as they finished.

Hashknife and Sleepy joined the three boys from the Tumbling H, and they went to the Welcome Saloon.

The K-10 horses were missing from the Greenback rack, which was conclusive evidence that Baldy had led his gang home. "Wouldn't have missed this evenin' for a fortune," declared Musical. "It was jist zip, boom, bang! Say, that Garcia shore is a knife-throwin' devil, ain't he? Pinned Baldy's wrist as nice as yuh please. Probably figured that his hand or arm was the only safe place to throw at to stop the shot."

"Makes me kinda twitch," admitted Ike. "Dang a knife! They kinda slither, don't they? If a feller ever comes after me with a knife, I'm goin' to plumb forget that I know how to do anythin', except run like hell."

"Shore a nasty thing," declared Cleve. "It ain't none of my business, Hartley, but I was wonderin' why yuh didn't let Baldy go ahead. Somebody has got to kill Torres."

"I reckon that's right," nodded Hashknife. "Somebody will have to kill him eventually, but I hope they'll kill him for somethin' that he done. Yuh see, he didn't kill Blair."

"I know it, but he tried to kill you."

"Yeah, but he didn't make good at it, Cleve."

"Oh, hell!" Cleve shrugged his shoulders and offered to buy a drink. "You argue jist like Big Medicine does. Take a chance like that to save a danged Mexican, who o'rt to be hidin' out from yore gun. I don't *sabe* yuh."

"I don't know that Torres tried to kill me, Cleve. There's a lot of folks that pack knives around here."

"Aw, don't argue with him," advised Sleepy. "He's got some awful queer notions in his head."

"I ain't goin' to," declared Cleve. "His notions may be queer, but his punch ain't. I vote that we go home."

"Home gits elected," stated Musical. "C'mon."

CHAPTER
NINE

FOUR MOUNTED MEN
AND A PACKHORSE

Twenty-four hours later, four mounted men, leading a packed horse, rode slowly through the brushy, broken hills near the border. They traveled in single file, the front rider leading the pack animal, with no sound except the soft creak of leather, or the faint "rip" of brush against boot and chap.

The feet of the horses were muffled with sacking, which left no tracks and also deadened their footfalls. It was as if a phantom caravan passed through the dimly lighted hills. There was no trail, but the leader picked his way unerringly, heading for the hills to the north, which separated them from Hawk Hole.

Somewhere a coyote sent up his plaintive cry, an eery sound in the silent hills. To the left of the leader a stick snapped and he jerked up his horse. The caravan stopped. The packhorse tried to nose past the leader, who swore softly and struck it across the nose with a rope end.

"All right," called the leader softly and started ahead.

From the left came the crashing report of a rifle, and the lead horse lunged forward, falling head first, throwing its rider into the brush. Another shot, and another, crashed out from the depths of the brush, while the other three riders whirled their horses out of the bottom of the swale, firing back at the flashes of powder.

The leader was running up the side of the slope, calling for one of the men to wait for him. The packhorse whirled and ran the opposite way, crashing through the brush. The hillside was flashing with rifle and revolver shots, although those in ambush were still keeping under cover and holding a decided advantage.

The riders were drawing farther away now. The leader had succeeded in mounting behind one of the other riders. Then they disappeared over the ridge and the firing stopped. The packhorse had crossed the ridge to the left, lunging through the heavy brush, trying to fight its way into open country, but a man ran out and grasped the flying rope, whirling the horse to a stop on the rocky slope.

Three more men swiftly gathered around the pack animal, and hurried it down through a cañon and out the other side, where four horses were tethered. They mounted swiftly and flogged the pack animal into a run, down across the broken slopes and onto a rutty road, which ran northwest into the hills.

As before the lead rider took care of the packhorse, while the rest bunched behind, swinging a rope end across the pack animal's rump at the least sign of slowing down.

There was nothing cautious about their progress. It seemed that above all things they desired speed.

Perhaps they were afraid that the other riders might intercept them, as they kept a close watch at the ridges to the north and east.

The reports of the rifle and revolver shots carried for a long way in that thin atmosphere, and attracted the attention of three other riders, who were following a trail farther to the west. After a hasty consultation they swung to the right and rode as swiftly as possible, heading northwest.

Straight up the rutty old road pounded the four men with the pack animal, heading for a low pass in the hills where the old road wound down to Pinnacle. They were almost to the summit, when the three riders flashed into view, coming swiftly down a broken hogback, clearly outlined against the sky.

The four men swore feelingly and urged the tired packhorse to greater speed. One of the three riders yelled at them, but the four riders and the pack animal swung into the downward road ahead, while the men from the hogback struck the road three hundred yards behind.

All the horses were weary from their uphill run, and there was little choice between the two factions in the race, except that those in the lead were hampered with the packhorse, which seemed disinclined to make it a runaway.

Near the bottom of the hill, and within half a mile of Pinnacle, the race swung to the left, circling the bottom of the hills and heading toward the Tumbling H Ranch. The three riders in the rear were around a series of sharp curves when those in the lead decided to make it a cross-country race, and as a result they raced past the turning-off place and lost valuable time in picking up the trail again.

The packhorse was giving its captors plenty of trouble now, and they took turns in beating it with rope ends to sustain speed. The pursuers were gaining a little because of this drawback, but were not near enough to make shooting accurate in that hazy light.

The chase swung nearer to the Tumbling H and the leaders circled slightly as if to head into the cañon at the rear of the ranch. Their horses were beginning to falter, and the pack animal was wheezing heavily.

The pursuers swung more to the right, taking advantage of the more open going, and their added speed caused the others to turn sharply toward the rear of the Tumbling H.

Unfortunately for the pursuers, they had swung too wide, passing the head of a deep washout, which angled in such a way that their course to the Tumbling H was blocked, and they were forced to swing back and lose much time in circling the head of it again.

Their quarry had disappeared at the rear of the Tumbling H, in the blocky shadows of the cañon mouth, forcing the pursuers to go carefully for fear of an ambush. It was several minutes later that the four riders came into view again, swinging back over a ridge several hundred yards away and heading in the general direction in which they had come.

The three riders swung their horses away from the Tumbling H, and again took up the chase into the hills. But the chase was of short duration this time. Only once, after crossing the ridge, did the pursuers get a glimpse of the other riders, and then they disappeared completely. So far away were they that the three riders drew up their jaded horses, swore to do better next time, and headed back toward the road.

While the pursuit went into the hills, Hashknife Hartley leaned out of their little window and listened. Sleepy was snoring loudly, unmindful of the thud of hoofs which had brought Hashknife to investigate.

He knew that the horses, had passed close to the corral although he had been unable to glimpse any of them. Softly he drew on his boots, buckled on his belt, and slid out through the narrow window, which was only a few feet above the floor.

Hashknife chuckled at his appearance and hoped that none of the Hawkworth family might awake and see him. He was clad in a gray suit of underwear, which had changed its original shape from many washings, a pair of boots, and a cartridge belt.

He went slowly out across the yard and around to the corral gate, scanning the hills for any sign of the horses which had passed. A chill wind was blowing, which Hashknife realized was not the best thing in the world for his rheumatism, and he was about to turn back when something inside the corral attracted his attention.

His investigation disclosed the fact that a weary-legged packhorse was standing in there, head hanging low, and showing every indication of having traveled far and fast. Hashknife spoke to the animal and examined the pack, which consisted of pack sacks, hung to a pack saddle and lightly covered with a tarpaulin, over which a diamond hitch had been thrown.

"Kinda queer," observed Hashknife to himself. "Somebody sure left this animal here in a hurry, so we better have a look."

Swiftly he took off the hitch, threw aside the tarpaulin, and lifted down the pack sacks. A short investigation showed him what the sacks contained. For several moments he debated. It was a dangerous cargo to be handling; worth a fortune in the right place. And the owners were sure to come back after it.

He picked up the two sacks, went through the corral gate and into the cañon, where he dumped the contents and came back with the sacks.

Hashknife knew how to throw the diamond hitch, and in a few minutes the animal was packed again, sans contents. The rawhide pack sacks held their shapes, and would have to be taken off the saddle before the lack of contents would be noted.

Then he went back back up the cañon and began disposing of what he had confiscated. It was considerable of a task to put it all away in the dark, and to obliterate all sign of the burying, and he was busy for the greater part of an hour.

And he was so busy that he did not see a man sneak around the corner of the barn, lead the horse out of the corral, and disappear. But he discovered the loss of the horse when he went back past the corral. The gate sagged open, creaking slightly in the wind. So he fastened it and went back to the house and crawled into

118

the window. Sleepy's snores still resounded in the little room, and Hashknife grinned widely to himself, as he snuggled down into the blankets.

"Somebody's goin' to swear real hard when they unpack that horse," he told himself. "And me, like a darn fool, got so blamed excited that I never even looked at its brand. All fools ain't dead yet, but one of 'em is feelin' twinges of rheumatics."

It was just at daylight that Baldy Kern, Jack Baum, Two-Fingers Kohler, and Ben Horan rode in at the K-10 Ranch. Baldy was mounted behind Jack Baum, and they were a disgruntled quartet of cowmen.

Kohler's right cheek was streaked with blood from a bullet furrow, and Ben Horan's ribs were still aching from a bullet, which had scored them. They dismounted and turned their horses into the corral.

Doctor Meline met them at the corral, and his expression showed that he was worried.

"Well?" he queried shortly.

"No 'Well' about it!" snapped Baldy. "C'mon in the house."

Meline followed him in, trailed by the others, and they sat down.

"Somebody got wise," said Baldy wearily. "We lost the stuff."

"You lost it!"

Meline almost screamed. He got to his feet and glared down at Baldy.

"You lost all that stuff, Kern?"

"Yeah."

"My God!" Meline looked foolishly around. "It — it was a fortune."

"Damn near misfortune," said Kohler. "An inch nearer and I wouldn't 'a' had any face left."

"Same here, and I'm ribless," complained Horan.

"Well, well!" said Meline nervously. "Tell me about it."

"There ain't much to tell," said Kern. "We got the stuff from Guadalupe and had it packed. We muffled the horses' hoofs and took the trail that Guadalupe picked out. Everythin' was fine until a little ways this side of the border, where we runs into an ambush.

"They downed my horse the first shot and the pack animal got away. I managed to get up behind Jack, but we didn't have a chance. They were in the brush, where we couldn't see 'em, and we were out in the open. We got away — thassall."

"And they got the packhorse, did they?" Meline paced the floor nervously. "Got away with a fortune!"

He turned to Baldy.

"Was it Government officers?"

"Hell, we didn't see nobody!" snappy Baldy. "I tell yuh it was all set for us, and we horned right into it. Do yuh suppose Steve Guadalupe double-crossed us?"

"Perhaps. Say, what about that greaser that brought us the note?"

"Felipe? Hell, no. He's half-witted. He wouldn't do anythin' crooked, 'cause he ain't got sense enough."

"All right."

120

Meline stopped pacing the floor and looked at the four men. Kohler swore softly and caressed his cheek. From the kitchen came the sound of the Mexican cook, banging the dishes as he prepared breakfast.

"Baldy, there is something wrong around here," said Meline coldly. "Somebody stole that letter I sent you, and somebody knew that our cargo was coming through that place tonight. There's a traitor, and the sooner we find out who it is the better."

"Not better for him, Doc," said Baldy angrily.

"You don't need to look at me, Doc!" snapped Horan. "If I was a traitor I wouldn't take a chance like that. I think too damn much of my ribs."

"Nobody's accusin' any of you boys," said Baldy. "You walked into the trap with me."

"Then where is he?" queried Meline. "He's on the inside of our deals. You don't know whether it was Government officers or not?"

"How could I? Still, they don't usually bushwack. I've got a hunch that somebody stole our cargo for themselves. Somebody knew that we were comin' across last night, that's a cinch. If it had been Government officers they would 'a' tried to nail us along with the stuff."

"Yes, that's true. Do you suppose it could have been the work of those strange cowboys?"

"It sure could," grunted Kohler, his hand going to his neck.

"Torres!" exploded Baldy. "By God, this is his work. He's in with Steve Guadalupe, and I'll bet he found out about that cargo. They're both Mex, damn 'em."

121

"Yes, and Hartley and Stevens are in with Torres," growled Kohler. "If they wasn't, why did they block us? I vote that we go and get them two smart punchers."

"But that doesn't prove that there is a traitor among us," said Meline. "Who got that letter? Torres had nothing to do with your mail, Baldy."

"Mebbe the letter was lost and Torres found it," suggested Horan.

"Hardly probable. What kind of a person was this Blair?"

"Blair was all right," said Baldy, adjusting the bandage on his wrist. "I sent Blair out to trail Torres and Garcia the night Blair was killed. Them two Mexicans went out of here, headin' south, but they must have circled and bushwacked Blair."

The Mexican cook announced breakfast, and they all trooped in to eat. The loss of the big cargo was a blow to Meline, who had paid for it in hard cash. He was still complaining about the loss of the money he had sent to Big Medicine Hawkworth, which he had only valued at five hundred dollars with the express company.

And he was half-afraid of Baldy Kern and his hard-riding crew. He could not bulldoze them, and he knew that their loyalty to him was only because of the fact that he paid well. It was true that Baldy Kern had an interest in the business, but dollars did not mean as much to Baldy as they did to Meline.

"What about Lee Yung?" asked Baldy, as they ate breakfast. "Can yuh trust him, Doc?"

"Why not? He lost as much as I did on the deal."

"If he wasn't in on it," suggested Baldy meaningly.

Meline shook his head. He did not believe that the Chinaman would double-cross him. The boys finished breakfast and rolled into their bunks for a sleep, while Meline sat down and tried to figure out who was trying to spoil his game; a game that was causing much concern among the customs inspectors and making big money for those actively interested.

CHAPTER
TEN

"THANK THE LADY!"

And at the same hour of the morning the Tumbling H outfit ate breakfast to the scratching music of "The Holy City," while Musical Matthews, a boot in each hand, sat before the old machine and drank in the song.

Hashknife had said nothing about the events of the night. Jack Hill was able to attend the meal, but said little. Since Big Medicine had upbraided him he had been sullenly silent, except when he had an opportunity to speak alone with Wanna.

As a result the boys of the Tumbling H ignored him. They had been considerate of him, but not friendly.

"Hair's too slick," declared Ike, and that seemed to be their general opinion.

But their indifference had little effect on Jack Hill, who looked upon them as a lot of uncouth louts, which, from his viewpoint, they probably seemed to be.

Breakfast was hardly over when three men rode up to the house and dismounted. Big Medicine saw them through the window, and he squinted wonderingly.

"Federal officers," he said. "Three of 'em."

He went to the door, followed by the other men. It was the first visit of the officers, three hard-bitten

124

border officers, Ed McGurk, Art Whaley, and "Skinner" Burns.

"Hello, Hawkworth," said McGurk, as his eyes searched the faces of Hashknife and Sleepy, knowing that they were strangers.

"Good morning, McGurk," replied Big Medicine easily. "Riding early, it seems."

"Does seem thataway," nodded the officer. "Rode a lot earlier than this — and others done the same."

"Yes? I don't quite understand you."

"I'm not talkin' riddles," said McGurk. "Mebbe yuh don't know what I mean, and mebbe yuh do. Last night" — McGurk shifted his belt a trifle, but kept his eyes on Big Medicine's face — "we chased three men and a packhorse, comin' from toward the border.

"They had the jump on us. We chased 'em here to yore place, where they gave us the slip long enough to make a getaway. We follered 'em over the ridge on the south side of the cañon, but lost 'em —"

"Interesting," said Big Medicine.

"Yeah, it is." McGurk was sarcastic. "Yuh remember I spoke about a pack animal? Well, when we gave up the chase, Skinner says he's sure they've ditched the packhorse. We decided to circle back this way and take another look, and we runs slap into a feller takin' the horse away from here, from yore ranch."

"From here?" queried Big Medicine wonderingly.

"Yeah, from here. But he seen us at the same time. The packhorse was too tired to run, so he cut loose and got away through a manzanita flat, but we got the pack animal."

"Well — and then what?" asked Big Medicine.

"The pack sacks were empty."

"Empty?"

"Yeah, empty! They wasn't empty when that horse was left here."

"How do yuh know?" asked Hashknife.

McGurk squinted closely at Hashknife.

"Who are you?" he asked coldly.

"Do yuh have to tell yore name in order to ask a question?"

McGurk spat angrily, while the Tumbling H boys grinned.

"I'll ask the same question, if you don't care to answer Mr. Hartley," said Big Medicine. "How do you know that the pack sacks weren't empty when the horse came to my ranch, McGurk?"

"Would them three men fight so hard for a getaway if there wasn't smuggled stuff on that horse?" demanded McGurk.

"Mebbe they stole the horse," suggested Sleepy.

"Na-a-aw, hell!" exploded Skinner Burns angrily.

"I've knowed horse-thieves to put up a hell of a race and a fight to get away," said Sleepy innocently.

"The hell yuh have," grunted McGurk. "You've been around quite a lot, ain't yuh?"

"Twice," said Sleepy.

"Around where?" asked Burns.

"Quite a lot."

"All right," said McGurk angrily. "This ain't gettin' us no place. We'll search the place, Hawkworth."

"Certainly, McGurk. The Tumbling H has nothing to conceal."

The three officers headed for the stable, while the men of the Tumbling H grouped together and followed them. They all knew, except Hashknife, that the officers were all wrong, and he felt sure that they would not find his cache.

Nor did they. After an hour of searching, which included the ranch-house, they were forced to admit that nothing had been overlooked. They were satisfied that the Tumbling H contained no contraband, but they were not contented.

"Yuh didn't overlook any place, didja?" asked Hashknife, when the officers came back to their horses.

"If we think of any place we didn't look, we'll come back," said McGurk peevishly. "You got away with it this time, I guess."

"Kinda looks like it," grinned Hashknife. "Mind tellin' us what was in them pack sacks?"

McGurk looked him over coldly. He wanted to make some cutting remark, but Hashknife's grin was too infectious. So McGurk grinned, although wearily, and mounted his horse.

"I don't know what was in 'em," he admitted. "I don't know whether there was anythin' in 'em or not. The rest of the story is just like I told it to you. Drugs are bein' run across the line in big bunches, and if any man deserves killin', it's a drug-runner. Lotsa times I can forgive a horse-thief or a murderer, but not a drug-runner."

"Same here," said Hashknife thoughtfully. "Officer, you've got the story pretty straight, but there's a few pages missin'. Go back to the border and try again next time. I reckon there'll be a next time."

"What do you mean?" queried McGurk.

"You'll have to guess," grinned Hashknife.

The three officers rode away, wondering what Hashknife meant, while the Tumbling H men lost no time in asking Hashknife what he meant. But Hashknife refused to say. He knew what it would mean to Big Medicine to have that cargo of drugs found on the Tumbling H, so he said nothing. Jack Hill, the invalid, heard what had been said, from just inside the front door, but asked no questions.

He went back to his seat in the shade at the rear of the ranch-house, where he re-read an old magazine. Hashknife, Sleepy, and Ike elected to spend their time at the corral, breaking a pair of colts, while Big Medicine, Musical, and Cleve saddled their horses and rode into the hills toward the border.

Wanna finished her work in the house and came outside, where Jack huddled in his chair and looked out across the hills. He smiled at her preoccupied expression and motioned for her to sit down beside him. She came closer, but did not sit down.

"What's the matter, little girl?" he asked.

"I don't know."

Wanna shook her head.

"I know." He laughed softly. "You're getting tired of living out here in the wilderness. I don't blame you. I think I'll go away about tomorrow."

"Tomorrow?" she asked quickly. "You going away?"

"Well" — he smiled crookedly — "I can't stay here any longer. Your father don't like me, Wanna."

"Why?"

"I don't know. He don't want me to talk to you."

"Don't he?"

Wanna turned and started for the door.

"Here!" he called to her. "Where are you going, Wanna?"

"I'm going away."

"Can you beat that?" wondered Jack aloud, addressing the wide world. "Come back here, you foolish girl. Your father can't expect to keep you from talking, can he? Come back and sit down."

Wanna stopped, but did not come back.

"Why don't my father want you to talk to me?" she asked.

"Oh, gosh, I don't know. What do we care? Come back here and I'll talk to you about San Francisco. Come on, Wanna. Your father won't be back for several hours, so it will be all right."

Wanna went slowly back. She did not want to disobey her father, but she did want to hear more of the wonders of the outside world. Finally she sat down beside Jack, forgetful of everything, except his word pictures of the places outside Hawk Hole.

Lucy came to the kitchen door, where she could hear the soft drone of voices from around the corner. She listened for several moments before going to the corner, where she could see Wanna and Jack, sitting close together, talking in undertones.

"Wanna!" said Lucy sharply.

The girl sprang to her feet and turned to look at her mother.

"Come, Wanna," said Lucy.

Wanna looked quickly at Jack, who threw his old magazine aside in disgust. Wanna went slowly to her mother, who motioned for her to go into the house. Jack turned and scowled at Lucy, his eyes snapping with anger.

"You, too, eh?" he snapped. "What harm is there for me to talk to the poor ignorant kid?"

"Big Medicine say no," said Lucy calmly. "You know that."

"Oh, all right!" disgustedly. "I'm about through with this place."

"You all through," said Lucy stolidly.

She turned and went down to the corral, where she called to Ike. He threw down his rope and came to her.

"You hitch up team," she said. "You take Jack Hill to town."

"All right," nodded Ike. "All well, now, eh?"

"Too damn well," said Lucy inelegantly, and went back to the house, where she confronted Jack again.

"You git ready," she said. "You go away right now."

"All right." He got to his feet and started for the house. "I'm good and ready to go, you bet. I never was as sour on any place in my life."

"This place sour for you now, you bet," said Lucy.

He whirled and glowered at her.

"I'll remember this," he told her.

Sleepy was coming up from the corral, but neither of them noticed him.

"Some day I'll show Big Medicine Hawkworth where to head in — and the rest of you."

"Me included?" asked Sleepy.

Jack turned his head. This was not so good. He turned to enter the house, but Sleepy stopped him.

"Thank the lady for what she's done for you," ordered Sleepy.

"I will, like hell!"

"I only ask once," said Sleepy warningly. "I hate to hit a cripple, but if you don't thank Mrs. Hawkworth for takin' care of you, I'll make you an invalid for the rest of your life — you dirty, low-down cur."

Sleepy was close to Jack, and coming closer. Instead of complying with Sleepy's order, Jack reached inside his coat. Sleepy dived into him, slamming him back against the door jamb, while he almost twisted Jack's right arm out of the socket in order to force him to drop a small pearl-handled revolver, which he had drawn from an inside pocket.

Sleepy flung him aside and kicked the gun out into the yard.

"Baby had a pretty tooth, didn't he?" mocked Sleepy. "Now, you cross between a polecat and another one, thank the lady."

Jack shrank back against the wall, panting with anger, while Sleepy waited for him to regain his breath. Then Jack thanked Lucy for her kindness to him. It was the only way out. He knew that Sleepy would make good his threat, and Jack felt that a live coward was worth several dead heroes.

Hashknife and Ike were coming up with the wagon, so Sleepy let Jack go in to pack up his few belongings. Hashknife picked up Jack's revolver and looked at it curiously.

"Shook it out of little 'Slick Hair'," said Sleepy. "He didn't want to thank Mrs. Hawkworth. Got real huffy and drawed his prize peashooter."

"Uh-huh."

Hashknife sniffed at the caliber of the gun and tossed it aside as something unclean.

"Gimme that," said Ike seriously. "I'll have a pin put on it and wear it in my necktie."

"To gaudy." Hashknife shook his head. "Smells of beauty powder."

Jack came out and climbed into the wagon, as Hashknife picked up the gun and examined it again.

"Whatcha lookin' for?" asked Ike.

"I'm lookin' for the manicure scissors in this darned thing."

Jack growled a soft oath, and Ike spoke excitedly to Hashknife. "He says there ain't none in it, Hashknife. It's a per-fume bottle. Ha, ha, ha, ha!

Ike kicked off the brake and they started for town. Lucy smiled at Sleepy and held out her hand.

"*Mahsie*," she said softly.

Sleepy shook hands with her thoughtfully. Then —

"*Kiwa teahwit*," he said.

It was the only Chinook he could remember, in response to her "Thank you."

He turned to Hashknife.

"Ain't we goin' to town, too?" he asked.

"Yeah," laughed Hashknife. "C'mon, old bowlegs."

After the border officers left the Tumbling H Ranch no wiser than before they came, they overtook Lon Pelly, the sheriff, and Cloudy Day, who were heading for Pinnacle. Pelly had not been able to find enough poker-players in Caliente, so he made it appear that urgent business called him to Pinnacle.

McGurk and Pelly were old friends, and, both of them being officers of the law, it was perfectly natural that McGurk should tell Pelly about their chase and disappointment. Pelly was both amused and sympathetic.

"Does look kinda funny," admitted Pelly. "Still there's lots of queer things happen in this neck of the woods, Mac. I've got so I don't believe anythin' I hear, and only half what I see."

"And that's about fifty per cent more than I do," said McGurk. "Maybe that packhorse didn't have nothin' on but the empty sacks. Maybe somebody just didn't want us to see who they were. There's a lot of maybes about it, Lon, but somethin' tells me that the pack sacks were loaded, and that somebody shifted the cargo on us."

"You'll get a lot of gray hairs worryin' about it," laughed Pelly. "I'd rather set back of some reds, whites, and blues on a green-covered table than to pack the red, white, and blue along that damn border. I could be knowed as a hell of a good sheriff, and die young."

133

"I guess that's right," grinned McGurk. "But either one is a good game when yuh win. I had a good hand last night, but somebody stole all the aces."

The revenue officers rode straight through Pinnacle, but the sheriff and deputy tied their horses at the Greenback rack and went into the saloon. The sheriff lost no time in getting a seat in a poker game, while Cloudy Day proceeded to regale his insides with his favorite beverage, which carried a high percentage of alcohol.

Baldy Kern, Two-Fingers Kohler, and Jack Baum rode in from the K-10. Baldy's wrist was heavily bandaged, and he wore his holster on the left side, which proved that Baldy was ambidextrous — or tried to be. Kohler explained that his cheek was cut from accidental contact with a barbed wire, which cut it did not resemble in the least.

Cloudy was fairly well "organized" when the K-10 outfit rode in, and they were not averse to helping him imbibe a few more. Cloudy's sense of humor grew greater with each successive drink, so it was not long before he laughed aloud at what McGurk had told them.

"What's funny?" asked Kohler.

"A revenue officer chasin' a empty packhorse."

"Empty packhorse?" queried Baldy.

"Yuh know what I mean — empty pack sacks."

Cloudy was almost crying with alcoholic mirth.

"Chasin' it where?" demanded Kohler.

Cloudy wiped his eyes on his sleeve and explained as well as he could what McGurk had told them. He drew

134

diagrams in the air with both hands and otherwise illustrated how McGurk, Whaley, and Burns had chased three riders and one pack animal almost all the way from the border to the Tumbling H Ranch.

He dilated on the fact that the packhorse had been left at the ranch, and how the officers, suspecting such a thing, had come back in time to capture the horse, but lost the man who was taking it away. And then he leaned against the bar and sobbed out the fact that the packhorse carried nothing but empty pack sacks.

Baldy, Kohler, and Baum laughed with Cloudy. They slapped him on the back and bought more liquor. Jim Reed came in from the Greenhorn country and joined them. Of course Cloudy had to tell the story all over again, with certain variations, and Jim Reed laughed.

Faro Lanning came from his private room at the rear of the building, and Cloudy felt obliged to tell the story to Faro. By this time his continuity was very bad, so he was prompted by Baldy, Kohler, and Baum, and Reed, who knew the story probably better than Cloudy did.

Faro listened attentively and joined in the inevitable laugh at the expense of the revenue officers. In fact the story went over so well that Cloudy wanted to hire a hall and charge a nominal admission. He was serious. So was Baldy.

The story meant much to Baldy. He knew that some outfit had got wind of their crossing with the big cargo, and had hijacked them out of it. He felt sure that the officers had heard the shooting and had run into the men who had ambushed him. But he was at a loss to understand who had removed the cargo from the pack animal.

He wondered if Big Medicine and his men were this outfit. It looked very much as if they had pulled the trick.

"Could it be that Torres is in with the Tumblin' H outfit, and they killed Blair to keep him from tellin' somethin'?" he asked himself.

It looked plausible. Anyway, it was worth thinking over.

A little later Ike Marsh drove in, bringing the disgruntled Jack Hill to town, and Jack Baum, looking from the saloon window, saw them stop in front of the hotel, where the stranger got out and went inside. Ike drove to a hitch-rack and tied the team.

Before he left the rack, Hashknife and Sleepy rode in and tied their horses at the same rack. Baum lost no time in telling Baldy about it.

"The young feller seemed to walk pretty good," said Jack.

"Probably quittin' the ranch," said Baldy. "I've got to see him as soon as I can. Yuh never can tell what he knows about that damn layout at the Tumblin' H."

"What about these three punchers?" asked Baum. "We owe 'em somethin' for that other deal, Baldy."

"Not yet," cautioned Baldy. "Sing small just now. We don't care what they think, *sabe?*"

The three cowboys from the Tumbling H came in and almost bumped into the three from the K-10. It was their first meeting since the escape of Torres, but

Baldy did not seem to hold any grievance. He grinned at Hashknife and invited them all to have a drink.

"How's the wrist?" asked Hashknife, after they had accepted the invitation.

"Pretty good," replied Baldy. "Healin' up fine. How's things at the Tumblin' H?"

"All right. Hello, Cloudy."

Cloudy Day recovered sufficiently to realize that these men had not heard his side-splitting tale, so he proceeded to tell it incoherently. Baldy watched Hashknife's face closely, while Cloudy managed to mumble out the main details, but the tall cowboy's expression told him nothing.

"Sounds all right," grinned Hashknife, after Cloudy subsided. "But what does he mean about the stuff bein' left at the Tumblin' H?"

"Search me," said Baldy. "All I know about it is what he's been tellin'. Wasn't the revenue officers out there?"

"Sure they was. They searched the ranch from top to bottom, while we sat around and wondered what it was all about."

"Somebody havin' a pipe dream," smiled Baldy. "Ever' once in a while them revenue officers do things like that."

"Always tryin' to put the deadwood on somebody," declared Jim Reed, who had moved in close to hear the discussion.

Hashknife looked at Jim Reed, and a grin widened his mouth.

"The last time I seen you," said Hashknife, "you was comin' out of Hawkworth's house on yore ear."

Reed flushed angrily, started a denial, thought better of it and moved away. He did not care to discuss such a painful affair, and had hoped that no one would ever know that Big Medicine had thrown him out.

"I thought that him and Hawkworth were good friends," said Baldy.

"I dunno anythin' about it, except that he came out on his ear. Mebbe that's a mark of friendship here."

"Not hardly," grinned Baldy. "Mebbe Jim Reed was tryin' to sell Hawkworth some minin' property. I see yuh brought the young feller back with yuh. Is he all right again?"

"Able to take care of himself," said Hashknife. "He don't weigh very heavy, as a man, Kern."

"Didja find out what he's doin' here, or what he intended to do here?"

Hashknife shook his head.

"No he didn't say. He's an ungrateful young pup, I know that much about him. Mrs. Hawkworth nursed him all this time, took care of him every minute, and he swore at her when he left. If his body was heavy enough to break his neck, he'd probably been hung long ago."

Baldy grinned at Hashknife's opinion of Meline's son, whether he agreed with Hashknife or not. Baldy sat down at one of the games and Hashknife drifted away to join Sleepy and Ike. None of them wanted to gamble or drink, and Pinnacle held little else to amuse them, so they decided to go home.

CHAPTER
ELEVEN

DOC MELINE'S SON

Baldy waited until the three men had gone back to the Tumbling H before leaving the game to go to the hotel. He found Jack in the little office, moodily reading an old newspaper and smoking. The office was empty, except for the young man, so Baldy lost no time in opening the conversation.

"Yo're Doc Meline's son, ain't yuh?" he asked softly.

Jack looked up quickly and considered this hard-faced cowpuncher, but did not reply.

"Thassall right," grinned Baldy. "Yore old man is out at the K-10."

"My father?"

"Yeah."

"What in hell is he doing out there?" demanded Jack.

"Well, he ain't askin' fool questions," retorted Baldy. "I'll pick yuh up after dark tonight. Be down at the other end of town about eight o'clock, will yuh?"

"Who are you?" asked Jack curiously.

"Baldy Kern."

"Oh. Eight o'clock, eh? I'll be there."

Baldy whirled on his heel and went out. In front of the Greenback he met Kohler.

"Didja see the son and heir?" grinned Kohler.

"Yeah, I seen him," growled Baldy.

"What kind of a rooster is he, Baldy?"

"He's fine." Baldy wrinkled his nose disgustedly. "Too damn bad that holdup jigger was such a bad shot. I hope Meline takes his damned offspring home with him, before somebody kills him."

Jack Baum joined them and they headed for the K-10. Baldy was anxious to tell Meline what he had heard about the lost cargo, and to see what plans they might formulate to recover it. Considering the fact that it was worth a fortune, Baldy was willing to make an effort to recover those lost packages.

Doctor Meline was anxiously waiting for news, and Baldy was in a position to deliver it. Meline listened to Baldy's narrative, as told by Cloudy Day, and jumped at conclusions.

"The Tumbling H did the job," he declared. "Torres is in with them. They headed straight for the Tumbling H, where they shook off the pursuit and left the cargo, which was removed by someone at the ranch.

"Possibly it was done by those new cowboys. They were probably in cahoots with the men who robbed the stage that night. Anyway, that cargo is at the Tumbling H. They will keep it hidden until the affair has died down, unless we get it."

Baldy told Meline about his son and of their agreement to meet at eight o'clock. The arrangement seemed to please Meline greatly.

"Jack might know more than we do about it," said Meline. "He is no fool, that boy."

140

"Ain't he ?" asked Baldy innocently,

"He is not," declared Meline warmly. "In fact he knows as much about this deal as I do. He's game too. Nobody heard him crying for assistance, did they? Kept his mouth shut, didn't he? Nobody knows who he is. Calls himself Jack Hill." Meline laughed softly. "Jack's all right, you bet. I trained him myself."

"All right," Baldy spoke disgustedly. "I'd hate like hell to have you train anythin' for me."

"You are entitled to your private opinion," said Meline coldly.

"I hope so," smiled Baldy. "What are we goin' to do about that stuff at the Tumblin' H?"

"Wait until we talk with Jack. If we make a foolish move, it might ruin our chances for any further work; and the game is too good right now for us to take a chance. I'd like to have a talk with Lee Yung. He might have some good ideas, Kern."

"Damn slant eye!" grunted Baldy.

"He's a square shooter, Kern."

"Aw, I suppose he is. I just don't like the breed."

Meline walked the length of the room, thinking deeply, while Baldy sat on the edge of the table, indolently smoking a cigarette. Meline halted near him and cleared his throat.

"Kern, I don't like your attitude," he said coldly. "You take exceptions to everything. I am at the head of this outfit. This ranch belongs to me. Lee Yung is my partner in everything, and I trust him implicitly. We pay you and your men well for everything you do, and you must remember that we can always hire men to take your places."

"Is that so?" Baldy laughed and shook his head. "No, yuh can't, Doc. You'd have to bring strangers down here and teach 'em the border. The revenue officers would watch 'em like hawks. Eventually yuh might put it over, but not for a long time. And in the meantime" — Baldy laughed softly — "we might not be idle. Yuh see, Doc, we know the tricks of the trade."

Meline scowled heavily, but was forced to admit that Baldy had the better of the argument.

"We can't afford to quarrel," declared Meline, anxious to square matters. "We'll wait for Jack. I wonder if you could get Lee Yung to come back with you."

"I can try," agreed Baldy. "We've got to figure this thing out some way, and if Lee Yung can plan as well as he can play poker, he's a wizard."

Hashknife was just a little worried. Cloudy Day's story spread the news, and Hashknife felt sure that the interested parties would suspect that the contraband was hidden on the Tumbling H.

He was not familiar enough with the stuff even to estimate its value, but felt that it was worth a good many dollars, if handled in the right way. And he was also sure that its original owners would leave no stone unturned to recover it. As far as the cargo itself was concerned he did not think they would be able to uncover it, but he was afraid of what they might do to some of the Tumbling H people.

Hashknife had never studied the smuggling game, but he knew that the smugglers were as desperate as rustlers or outlaws of any other description.

Big Medicine did not comment on the fact that their star invalid was missing. Lucy had explained why she had sent him to town — which Big Medicine had told her to do, in ease he talked with Wanna again — and the explanation was satisfactory to Big Medicine.

Wanna said nothing. She did not understand why Jack had been sent from the ranch. Hashknife was curious to find out her opinion, but she shook her head sadly and went about her work.

Big Medicine and Hashknife spent the evening on the front steps of the ranch-house, smoking and talking about Hawk Hole. In an offhand way Hashknife mentioned Jim Reed.

"Did you see him today?" asked Big Medicine.

"Yeah," smiled Hashknife. "I mentioned the fact that you threw him out on his ear."

Big Medicine smoked slowly, thoughtfully.

"He used to come out here real often," he said. "I liked Jim. Jim owned a mine back in the Greenhorns, and I was going to buy a half interest. I had seen it and tested the ore. That package which was stolen from the stage was the money to buy a half interest in that mine, Hartley.

"It looked like a good proposition to me. I was to take half interest, and between us we were going to put up a stamp mill. Jim was to come out, fix up the papers, and then leave for the outside to buy the machinery. I was leaving it all to him.

143

"The day before the money was due, I met a prospector from the Greenhorns." Big Medicine knocked the dottle from his pipe and began filling it again. "From that prospector I learned that Jim Reed never owned a mine. He was merely showing me another man's property, going to sell me a half interest in something he did not own. And he was going to take my money, leave me a worthless piece of paper, and never come back to Hawk Hole again.

"He came out here to complete the deal, and I told him what I had learned. He denied it all, of course. In fact he became indignant, slapped his paper on the table and demanded that I keep my end of the bargain. I kept it, by throwing him out. That is the last I have ever seen of Jim Reed."

"What about the paper?" asked Hashknife anxiously. "Didja see it?"

Big Medicine laughed shortly.

"I kept it, Hartley. It was just several sheets of blank paper, folded together."

Hashknife laughed softly and began rolling another smoke. "I have a suspicion that Jim Reed is crooked," he said.

"Everything points that way," admitted Big Medicine.

The talk drifted to things along the border and Hashknife asked him if he knew Steve Guadalupe.

"I have only seen him once," said Big Medicine. "Guadalupe is afraid to cross the border. It is five years since he was on this side — at least, openly. He hates the whites, but they say he will do anything for gold.

144

"He's a small man, Hartley. Steve Guadalupe is not much over five feet tall, but inside his dirty brain is all the deviltry, cunning, and avarice of the low-bred Mexican and Yaqui combined.

"The Rancho Sierra is isolated; an ideal place for him to offer as a hangout for every type of outlaw. The Mexican Government is too busy with its own troubles to bother with him, and he is careful to keep out of the clutches of the men on this side.

"I have no doubt that Guadalupe is in constant touch with men in this part of the country. Many of the Tumbling H cattle have gone to fill the coffers of Guadalupe, and to fill the bellies of him and his men. I should like to wring his neck."

"Might be a pious deed," agreed Hashknife. "I wonder if the K-10 lost any cattle?"

"I don't know. There is no friendship lost between the Tumbling H and the K-10, so we should not be informed of their losses."

Big Medicine did not quiz Hashknife about what had been said to the revenue officers that morning, nor was Jack Hill mentioned. They finished out their smokes and went into the house, where Musical was trying to improve on the phonograph patents.

That night Hashknife and Sleepy sat in the corral, where Sleepy shivered in the chill wind and swore at himself for being partner to a lunatic.

Nothing happened, except for the wailing of a few wandering coyotes and the peevish hooting of an owl, far back in the dark cañon. Finally Hashknife decided that it was useless to stay longer, so they went back, crawled through the window, so as not to disturb anyone, and went to bed.

"I know one thing that I wasn't sure of before," declared Sleepy, as he snuggled down into bed.

"What's that, cowboy?" asked Hashknife.

"I know," said Sleepy drowsily, "that there's two fools in Hawk Hole, and you're both, Hashknife."

"I wouldn't be surprised if you was right," sighed Hashknife.

And while Hashknife lay awake trying to puzzle out some of the mysteries of Hawk Hole, Doctor Meline, Jack Meline, Lee Yung, and Baldy Kern sat in the K-10 ranch-house debating over their next move.

Jack had overheard Hashknife's conversation with McGurk, which proved to them that Hashknife knew something of the missing cargo. But Jack was unable to say whether or not the Tumbling H crew had been away from the ranch that night.

His room had been nearer the front of the house, but he thought that no one could move about in the house without making much noise, because of the creaking floors and stairs. He had heard no conversation which might connect them in any way with the hijacking.

"Hartley is our man," declared Doctor Meline. "He knows."

"And he is no fool," said Lee Yung.

"And I'd like to pay him back for that deal the other night," said Baldy, indicating his bandaged wrist. "But I don't know just how to work it. Hartley is no fool, that's a cinch."

146

"We could force him to tell," suggested Jack.

"If we had the chance," said Lee Yung softly. "Not being a fool, he may not give us the chance. Still, one can never tell what the gods have written, and it is well to have a plan, in case the gods should be kind to us."

"The gods don't mean much to me," said the practical Baldy. "Just give me a chance. To hell with the gods."

The hired men on the Tumbling H were never overworked. Big Medicine was no slave-driver, and let the cowboys plan out most of their own work. Musical opined that the corral needed a lot of repairs. He did not fancy riding around in the heat.

Cleve thought they really should investigate some of the water holes hack in the hills. Ike thought that somebody ought to go to Pinnacle after the mail. Being of different minds, they let Ike go to town while Cleve and Musical sat down at a four-handed poker game with Hashknife and Sleepy.

None of them having much money, they "owed" the game. It was uneventful, and lasted most of the day. In fact it lasted so long that they grew disgusted with each other, and finally went out to the corral, where they saddled a steer.

Steer riding may not sound eventful, but any bronc rider will tell you that a bucking steer is harder to stick to than a bucking horse. They solemnly drew straws to select a rider, and the lot fell to Sleepy, who protested that he had been framed.

"If you're afraid —" suggested Musical.

147

"It ain't that," replied Sleepy. "It's the principle of the thing."

"It don't look like it had much," grinned Hashknife, looking the steer over.

It was a white-faced animal, long legged, evil eyed. Sleepy tightened his belt and spat reflectively.

"Somebody pick out a soft place for him to land," said Cleve, snubbing a rope around his hip. "If yuh find yourself goin' plumb out of the State, Sleepy, cut the cinch. That saddle belongs to me."

"Yore saddle don't mean nothin' to me," grunted Sleepy. "Such things are below me, cowboy."

They had the steer snubbed close to a post, and held it until Sleepy had adjusted himself in the saddle. Musical kicked open the gate, while Hashknife slacked the rope enough to slip it off.

Then the three cowboys raced for the corral fence, where they perched on the top pole and hugged their knees.

For several moments the steer stood still, its back humped, its nose close to the ground. Then it bawled shudderingly, a deep-toned wail, as though the sins of the world might be weighing upon its mind.

And then it moved so suddenly that Sleepy was almost unseated. Once around that dusty corral went the gyrating steer, lunging against the sides of the corral, bucking in its own peculiar, side-wheel way, and finally headed out through the open gateway.

Big Medicine and Lucy were on the front steps, watching the fun. Perhaps the steer had never done any bucking before, but it was wise, resourceful, and very wicked. So it picked out Big Medicine and Lucy as being part and parcel to this ignominy, and headed for them, still bucking and bawling.

Big Medicine and Lucy beat a retreat inside the doorway, while the steer sheered off slightly, just as a horse and rider came around the corner. It was McGurk, the revenue officer, who had ridden up unobserved from that side of the ranch-house, and had moved into view right in the path of the bucking steer.

McGurk and his horse were not a dozen feet away from the bucking steer, which was also covering distance at a rapid rate, and running blind, with its head nosing the dirt. And almost before McGurk could realize what was going on Sleepy threw up both hands, collided with McGurk, and was knocked backwards into a stunted rosebush, when the steer elected to be under McGurk's mount.

The impact was so great that the big steer lifted the horse off its feet, dumping McGurk out of the saddle, and upending the frightened horse on its head, while the steer, minus the saddle, the cinch of which had snapped at the impact, went bawling into the hills.

Hashknife, Cleve, and Musical came running from the corral, while McGurk's horse got to its feet and trotted in a circle, as if undecided which way to go.

McGurk got to his feet, spitting sand and profanity, while Sleepy, his feet elevated in the rosebush, looked up at them with a vacant stare and tried to argue with them over the climate of Puget Sound.

"He's all right," grinned Hashknife. "That wallop knocked him back one season, but he'll catch up."

"McGurk, you picked a bad time to come around that corner," said Big Medicine seriously.

McGurk rubbed the back of his head and sat down on the steps.

"I didn't have a chance," he explained. "That damn steer was into me like a shot."

Sleepy was sitting up now, and Musical began singing softly:

"To-o-o-re-e-e-e-adore, don't spit on the floor; use the cuspidor, what do yuh think it's fo-o-o-er?"

"You think yo're damn smart, don't cha?" wailed Sleepy. "My God, how did I know that London Bridge was fallin' down?"

"Serves yuh right," declared Hashknife. "You knowed danged well it wasn't the right thing to do, Sleepy. Evry time yuh do wrong, yo're goin' to run into the law."

"Yeah, run into the law," complained McGurk, twisting his head to find out if it was still movable. "He sure ran into me. One of my legs is inches longer than it was, and my head popped when it hit the dirt."

McGurk got to his feet and walked over to his horse, which was being held by the grinning Cleve.

"Don't run away," said Big Medicine. "Supper is almost ready, and we'd like to have you eat with us."

"Well, I dunno." McGurk squinted at the setting sun and handed the rope back to Cleve. "I suppose I might as well, thanks. A little settin' down won't hurt me none. By grab, I sure shook myself awhile ago."

"I'm sorry I shucked yuh loose," grinned Sleepy painfully. "But yuh see, my steer wasn't no hurdle

150

racer. I had aplenty. Hereafter I may eat it, but I'll be darned if I ride it."

"Yuh made a good ride," complimented Musical. "Ain't many riders in this country that'll stick as long as you did. I'm glad I didn't get the short straw."

"That's the straw that almost broke several backs," said Hashknife.

They were just starting in to supper when Ike came into sight, riding furiously. He drew up his horse at the steps and spat out his information in one word —

"Rustlers!"

CHAPTER
TWELVE

"SAVE ME A PIECE OF HIS HIDE"

Cleve and Musical did not wait for any further information, but raced for the stable.

"Where are they?" asked Big Medicine anxiously.

"They cut the Greenhorn road near Smoky Cañon," panted Ike. "Olsen had been to Greenhorn and seen 'em on his way back. He said he couldn't swear that it was Tumbling H cattle, but there ain't no other brand in that range."

"Heading for the border?" asked McGurk.

"Yeah."

Hashknife and Sleepy raced for the stable, while Big Medicine went into the house. They saddled Big Medicine's horse and joined him at the front steps, where he was examining three rifles. It was not more than ten minutes after Ike's arrival until the seven men were riding away from the ranch-house, while a hot supper went to waste.

They swung to the west of Pinnacle and struck the road near where the three men and the packed horse had left it. About halfway to the summit the road branched. Big Medicine drew up for a consultation. It was about three miles from there to where the road swung in around the head of Smoky Cañon.

"What's the best bet?" asked Hashknife.

"There's no use going to Smoky Cañon," declared Big Medicine. "The cattle were passing there, and must be a long ways from there now. Unless I'm mistaken, they are heading for the border near the Rancho Sierra."

"Then let's try and cut them off," suggested McGurk.

They spurred on over the hill, following the old road. Darkness came down before they reached the border, and they rode slowly, listening for sounds of the herd.

"How big was the bunch of cattle?" asked Cleve.

"He didn't say," replied Ike. "He just said it was a big bunch."

Big Medicine swore at the darkness as they moved along. Unless they ran into the herd there was no chance of finding them. It would be several hours before moonlight, and there was a possibility of the rustlers being able to cross the border in the dark.

Mile after mile they followed the border, working westward, but they saw no cattle. It was too dark for them to detect the trail of a big herd, even if the cattle left tracks on that hard ground. They swung back, working slowly, and passed the point where they had come down.

Midnight came and found them still hunting. It was moonlight now, but they were little better off.

"It's no use," declared Big Medicine. "They've got all the best of it, so I'll have to swallow the dose and go home."

"Kinda looks like it," agreed McGurk. "I'll get the boys out early in the mornin' and swing down this way. Good night."

He rode away toward the west, while the Tumbling H crew disgustedly turned their weary horses and went back toward Hawk Hole.

"It is some of Torres' work," declared Big Medicine. "If I ever get a chance I'll break his neck. He thinks he is safe in running my cattle across to the Rancho Sierra, but someday I'll go down there and make him pay for every head he stole."

"You'll have company," said Ike glumly. "I've always wanted to go down there and whip me some Mexicans."

"They're not all bad, are they?" asked Sleepy.

"Not at all," replied Big Medicine. "There are some mighty good men in Mexico — lots of 'em. I suppose they average as well as any other race, but the types which frequent the border are the scum of both sides. A bad Mexican is a terror, but a bad white man is worse. We've got 'em both down here."

They swung down into the valley in sight of the lights of Pinnacle and turned to the left, following about the same trail as that taken by the chase two nights before.

There were no lights in the ranch-house. They stabled their horses, after Big Medicine had gone into the house, and were halfway to the house when Big Medicine called to them.

Wanna and her mother were not at the ranch-house, which had been ransacked from top to bottom. The rooms were strewn with everything, and boards had been pried up from both living-room and kitchen floors.

"There has been no rustling," said the Big Medicine weakly. "It was a ruse to get us away from the ranch."

"But where are the women?" asked Ike.

"They are not here," said Big Medicine hoarsely.

He was holding the lamp in one of his big hands, which trembled nervously.

"But — but why were they taken?" faltered Musical. "Who would take them away, Big Medicine?"

The big man shook his head and went from room to room, with the five cowboys following him. Everything indicated that the searchers had left nothing untouched. The drawers of an old dresser in Big Medicine's room had been emptied in a pile and the drawers thrown aside. The bedding was strewn widely, and even the pictures were torn down and kicked aside.

They came back to the living-room and sat down, silently wondering who had done this thing. Big Medicine did not rave nor curse. He only wondered in a painful way. Hashknife alone knew that the work had been done by the men who had lost that valuable cargo of drugs, and he felt responsible for Big Medicine's loss.

"What can we do?" wondered Cleve aloud. "There's no use in runnin' around."

"No use." Big Medicine shook his head. "They probably saw us ride away, and it gave them plenty of time."

His big bands clenched convulsively, and Hashknife wondered how long the ordinary man would live in the clutches of Big Medicine in his present frame of mind.

155

"No use," echoed Musical.

He got to his feet and crossed to the phonograph. The record case had been emptied, the records smashed. He picked up two pieces, which fitted together, and looked them over before holding them out for inspection.

"They sure knocked hell out of 'The Holy City,' " he said.

No one even smiled. Musical did not mean to be funny. He placed the pieces tenderly on the table, his eyes saddened as he looked at them.

"I sure liked that piece," he said simply.

"I know you did, Musical," said Big Medicine.

It seemed as if he had forgotten his own troubles to sympathize with Musical.

"Do yuh think that Torres done this?" queried Hashknife.

"I don't know," said Big Medicine.

"But what did they expect to find in here?" asked Cleve. "I don't *sabe* why they tore everythin' to pieces like this."

"Money," said Big Medicine. "They thought I kept it hidden, I suppose."

Hashknife wondered if someone had been looking for money. If that was it, he felt better about it. He decided to keep quiet about the hidden drugs, and see how things worked out.

It was a long wait until daylight, but they realized that nothing could be done in the dark. They breakfasted on a pot of coffee, mounted their horses, and headed for Pinnacle.

156

"What's our first move?" asked Hashknife.

"I don't know," replied Big Medicine. "I want to find Olsen and choke the truth out of him. Perhaps he did not lie, but it sounds like a scheme to get us away from the ranch."

They dismounted in town and went on a hunt for Olsen. The town was hardly awake, but they found that Olsen had not been there that night. They did not spread the news of what had taken place at the Tumbling H, because they knew it would do no good.

From a man at the Greenback Saloon they found that the sheriff and deputy were asleep at the hotel, after a night of poker. Hashknife mentioned Lee Yung, but the man had not seen him. They realized that they had not eaten a meal since noon of the previous day; so they went into a restaurant and had a meal.

The proprietor remembered that Jim Reed had been there with Olsen about six o'clock the night before, and they had gone away together. The proprietor remembered Hashknife as the man who had ducked Torres in the blacksmith's slack tub, and told him that he had seen Torres the evening before.

"What was he doin' here?" asked Hashknife.

"He wasn't in here. I live out of town a little ways, and I took some stuff out to the house about supper time. Torres rode past just after I got to the house. I guess he didn't stay, 'cause I didn't see him again."

They paid their checks and went outside.

"Olsen and Reed together," said Big Medicine. "Torres passes here about the right time. Torres is our man."

157

"And Olsen and Reed are in with him." Thus Ike vehemently.

"Wait a minute," said Hashknife. "I want to find out somethin'."

He hurried across the street and into the hotel, where he found the proprietor scrubbing out the office.

"Is that young Jack Hill here yet?" asked Hashknife.

The man wrung out his mop, spat reflectively, and shook his head.

"Nawsir, he ain't. Engaged a room and never used it. Walked out of here the night he came, and I ain't see hide nor hair of him since."

"Don't know where he went, do yuh?"

The man scratched his head and leaned the mop handle against his hip.

"No. Ike Marsh unloaded him here, yuh remember? Little later on I hears voices down here. So down I comes and sees Baldy Kern jist goin' away. I asks the young feller what Baldy wanted, but he don't seem to know who I mean. But at that, I reckon Baldy was a-talkin' to him."

Hashknife thanked him for the information and went back to the hitch-rack where the rest were waiting.

"We've decided to cross the border and visit the Rancho Sierra," declared Ike jubilantly. "Here's where I git me a Mexican. C'mon."

"Just a moment," begged Hashknife, and turned to Big Medicine. "Don't do anythin' rash until we have to, Hawkworth. There's a few things I'd like to look into first. For instance, I think that me and Sleepy will take a little ride out to the K-10."

158

"To the K-10? What is the idea, Hartley?"

"To satisfy my curiosity. They haven't anythin' against me and Sleepy, so we'll go out and have a talk with Baldy. Just kinda drop in, tell him about the rustlin', and advise him to keep his eyes open, *sabe?*"

"And what will we do all this time?" asked Musical. "I'm honin' to make somebody pay for this deal."

"Wait here," suggested Hashknife. "You may hear somethin' that will help us out a lot. We'll make the trip as fast as we can."

Big Medicine nodded doubtfully. He was anxious to head for the Rancho Sierra, but was willing to listen to reason.

"That's fine," grinned Hashknife. "You wait here and say nothin'. Mebbe Olsen will show up, and if he does, save me a piece of his hide. C'mon, Sleepy."

The K-10 outfit had not decided on just what to do. Half the night had been spent in planning, but no decision had been reached. It all depended on Hashknife. Lee Yung intended to go back to Pinnacle after breakfast and stay there until there was need of his services.

It was Kohler who first saw Hashknife and Sleepy coming. They were half a mile away, and Kohler was not sure of their identity, but the sharp eyes of Jack Meline detected the horses long before the identity of the riders could be learned. "Right into the net," grinned Baldy. "Talk about fate."

"The gods have decided," declared Lee Yung.

Jack Baum was down at the corral, so they did not call him. Kohler flattened himself against the wall near the door, a rifle in his hands, while the rest took points of vantage. Doctor Meline peered between the curtains at a front window, while Baldy stood at another — an open one — sixshooter ready.

Hashknife and Sleepy dismounted and came toward the door. Jack Baum saw them and called from the corral. They saw Sleepy stop and turn toward the corral, just as Hashknife knocked.

"Come in," said Baldy, cocking his gun.

Hashknife swung the door open and stepped half inside, blinking from the strong light outside, and before he could distinguish objects inside the room, Kohler brought the rifle barrel down across his head and Hashknife crumpled to the floor.

Sleepy heard the blow and saw Hashknife fall. The door slammed in his face and he sprang back, reaching for his gun, but Baldy fired from the open window and Sleepy went sprawling.

Jack Baum came running from the corral, stopped long enough to look down at Sleepy, and dashed into the house. Baldy whirled from the open window, holding his smoking gun, and laughed loudly.

"Got him," he said, indicating the open window.

He walked over to Hashknife and looked down at him, his face registering great satisfaction. Lee Yung was on his knees beside Hashknife, examining his head.

"Not hurt much," said the Chinaman. "He'll wake up in a few minutes."

Kohler grinned with satisfaction and stepped back to the window. His expression changed and he darted for the door, mouthing a curse. He flung open the door and stepped out, swinging up his rifle.

There was only one horse in the yard and no dead man. About two hundred yards down the road went Sleepy, riding madly toward Pinnacle. Kohler threw up his rifle and emptied the magazine in a wild attempt to drop either horse or rider, while Baldy ran out to Hashknife's tall gray and mounted hurriedly. He was going to try and overtake Sleepy.

But he reckoned without the gray, which only admitted of one master. Baldy had hardly settled in the saddle when the gray whirled wildly and lunged into a bucking orgy that was a revelation even to those hard riders.

Baldy stayed five jumps and then went end over end, falling on his hands and knees, skinning his chin and otherwise paying well for his temerity. Baldy's gun went spinning away, while the tall gray trotted down toward the corral, holding up its head to keep from stepping on the reins.

Jack Baum helped Baldy to his feet. The boss of the K-10 looked as if he had stuck his chin against a grindstone, and his knees and hands were badly bruised. He staggered into the house and flopped into a chair, while Lee Yung brought water and towels.

"This is a hell of a mess!" wailed Baldy. "Stevens has gone back to town, and we'll have the whole damn works on our trail."

161

"You shot him, didn't yuh?" asked Kohler. "You said yuh did."

"I seen him fall," declared Baum. "I didn't know what it was all about. He sure fell like he was killed."

"He was a wise man," said Lee Yung. "Knowing that the odds were against him, he fell down. And we, like fools, accepted what he gave us."

"We've got to get out of here," said Meline nervously.

"We sure have," agreed Baldy. "Tie that damn fool tight and somebody bring his horse. Get plenty of ropes. For God's sake, move fast, can'tcha? This is no time to gawp."

And while the K-10 moved swiftly, Sleepy Stevens left a screen of dust behind him, as he pounded along the road. He had felt the sting of Baldy's bullet, which had burned his neck, and had dropped flat, feeling that his complete collapse would stop further shooting.

As soon as Baum had gone inside the house, Sleepy had run to his horse, mounted, and headed for town. It was not cowardice on his part. He knew that it would be impossible for him to fight that outfit single-handed, especially as they were protected by the walls of the ranch-house, so he went for help.

Owing to the fact that he had escaped, he did not think they would kill Hashknife. It might have been a different story if they had caught both of them. Knowing that he would report against them, they might be afraid to do anything rash.

He raced in to Pinnacle and found the Tumbling H men in the Greenback Saloon. Without exciting too much suspicion he drew them aside and hurriedly told

162

them what had happened. The sheriff and deputy were in a poker game, but they did not bother to enlist their services.

They mounted and rode swiftly out of town toward the K-10, while Sleepy gave the details of what had happened.

"Mebbe I'll git me a white man," gritted Musical. "Gimme one li'l chance to notch a sight on any of that bunch. If one of them sons of guns busted that record, I'll borry his ears."

Regardless of the fact that there might be desperate men inside the K-10 buildings, the five riders spurred their horses almost to the front steps, dismounted hurriedly, and smashed in the front door.

But except for a frightened Mexican cook, the place was deserted. Sleepy pinned him against the wall and promised to shoot the ears off his head if he did not tell them where everyone had gone, but the Mexican did not know.

Musical talked to him in his own language, but all Musical could get from him was a protestation that he knew nothing, except that they had tied a wounded man to a horse and had all ridden away. No, he did not know their direction nor destination.

They let him go and went back to their horses. The K-10 corral was empty. Sleepy leaned dejectedly against the shoulder of his horse and squinted out across the hills.

"Darn his long-legged soul," he said hoarsely, blinking into the sun. "Went and run his head right into a trap. Never did have any sense, dang him. Now he's

163

up against a tough deal, and here I am, standin' here in the sun, like a danged galliwimpus. It kinda seems" — Sleepy hesitated — "Me and him have been together so long that I've let him do my thinkin'."

"Well," said Big Medicine wearily, as he swung his leg across his saddle, "it sems like a lot of things have gone wrong. I haven't the slightest idea where the K-10 outfit have gone."

"Mexico!" snapped Ike angrily.

He wanted to invade the country.

"Perhaps," nodded Big Medicine. "I suppose we may as well tell the sheriff and enlist his help."

"And have him tell us that it's all wrong to go across the border," grumbled Musical. "We don't need his help. Anyway, he's prob'ly in a big pot jist now and won't want to be bothered."

They rode slowly away from the K-10 and headed back toward Pinnacle. Sleepy humped in his saddle and pictured what he would do when he met any of that K-10 outfit. The loss of Hashknife had driven away his habitual sense of humor, and all he wanted to do was to find something or somebody to shoot at.

CHAPTER
THIRTEEN

GONZALES

The Rancho Sierra had long been the rendezvous of the *contrabandista*, a sanctuary for outlaws of every type and description for many years. Steve Guadalupe welcomed them all, took their gold freely, and asked no questions.

Situated in the heart of the hills, half-hidden by the overhanging bluff against which it had been built, and commanding a view in three directions, it would be impossible of undetected approach, except at night.

The ranch-house was an L-shaped, one-story adobe structure, and so weathered with age that it seemed part of the bluff, which was covered with a growth of mesquite and manzanita. South of the ranch-house extended a long, low, adobe shed, surrounded on the west by a big pole corral, capable of holding many horses.

The ranch-house was roomy, with thick walls, and the windows were barred, like those of a prison. The floor of adobe had been walked upon until it was flintlike in texture, and the furnishings were of the most crude construction.

In one end of the L was the kitchen, where a frowsy old Mexican, overalled, half-shirted, barefooted, cooked food in big black kettles in an open fireplace. There was little idea of sanitation. The floor of the kitchen reeked of ancient spillings. Strings of chili peppers hung in festoons from the ceiling, a half-eaten haunch of venison on the table attracted a myriad of flies, while more of the insects buzzed about the head of the half-asleep cook.

In the angle of the L, facing each other across a rough table, on which stood a bottle of mescal and two tin cups, sat Pedro Torres and Steve Guadalupe. Big Medicine's description fitted Guadalupe well. His dirty gray hair, matted in some spots and in others standing upright like a handful of foxtail grass, framed a thin, evil countenance, aged to the texture of dirty parchment, almost belying the brilliancy of his two little eyes, which age had failed to dim.

His mouth was wide and the lips so thin that it appeared more like a gash than a mouth. His raiment was little better than that of his cook, except that his shoulders were draped with a bright-colored serape, and on the index finger of his right hand he wore a huge emerald ring.

His general appearance was a direct contrast with that of the dapper Torres, who was drinking almost too much of the potent liquor to suit Guadalupe. Guadalupe drank litle. He swept the bottle off the table and shoved it inside his serape.

"*Idiota!*" he snarled.

"*Ladron!*" snapped Torres, reaching across the table, motioning for Guadalupe to return the bottle.

166

"You are a fool," declared Guadalupe in Spanish. "You drink so much you cannot talk sense."

"The bottle," ordered Torres harshly.

Guadalupe grinned and put it back on the table.

"That is as it should be," muttered Torres, somewhat mollified. "I pay well, do I not, Steve?"

"Of that I am always sure," grinned Guadalupe. "Few men fail to pay Guadalupe. Some have failed to pay — in gold."

Torres gulped another drink and nodded vehemently.

"But they paid, eh, *compadre?* Oh, you know how, my friend. Guadalupe is no fool."

"When you say it, I wonder," grinned Guadalupe. "But I do not like your scheme, Torres. A priest is not a good thing to bring to the Rancho Sierra. None have ever entered, although there have been times when —"

Guadalupe crossed himself piously and grinned at Torres.

"Nor have I ever paid for many candles," grinned Torres. "I have never felt the need. But this is different."

"Fool!" grunted Guadalupe. "You have the girl. Marriage is only for those who are too weak to steal and keep a girl. You have stolen her. Are you afraid to hold her?"

"I fear nothing. To steal a girl is nothing. I have done it before, my friend. But" — Torres poured out a fresh drink — "I want to stand up before a priest and laugh. Ha, ha, ha ha! I want this girl for my wife, do you understand? I want it known that she is the wife of Torres."

"Revenge, eh?" smiled Guadalupe. "To laugh at someone, you are willing to marry what you might have without marriage. Is that it, Torres?"

"That is for me to know. I am willing to pay one hundred dollars in gold, Guadalupe. Bring me a priest. Somewhat we will find someone to play the guitar, the mandolin. We will open a cask of wine, while Lopez roasts us much meat, and we will hold a marriage *fiesta* at the Rancho Sierra."

Torres staggered to his feet and slapped Guadalupe on the back.

"The first marriage in the Rancho Sierra, eh, old one? What care we for the blabbing tongues of the priests? What harm could they do to us? Send Felipe to Santa Isabella and have him bring back a mumbling priest to say his words over Torres and his bride."

"It will not take him more than a night and a day. Drink one more cup of mescal, old wolf. Warm up your cold bones. Where is Felipe, the half-wit? Call him. We waste time, and the bridegroom waits."

They drank another cup of the mescal, holding their cups high above their heads in a leering toast. Torres was getting drunk. Guadalupe flung his cup aside, upset the bottle to see if it contained any more liquor, and started toward the door to call Felipe.

Lopez shuffled in swiftly from the kitchen.

"Gonzales," he said warningly.

Torres swore feelingly and leaned against the table. He did not want Gonzales to come now — Gonzales, the unprincipled pig of a ruffian, who supplied Guadalupe with the goods which were to be smuggled;

Gonzales, whose mustaches reached below his chin, and who wanted to fight after the second drink of *tequila*.

Guadalupe swung open the door and blinked into the sunlight. The huge Gonzales, resplendent in a red silk shirt, the widest and tallest hat he had been able to purchase, leather breeches, and heavy hoots, while his waist was circled by an ornate cartridge belt, which sparkled with silver trimming and brass cartridge heads, stood near, holding a weary-looking horse.

There were two more wide-hatted Mexicans with him, also heavily armed, and two mules packed. Felipe, the half-wit, was waiting for Gonzales to hand him the bridle reins. The air was dusty from the trampling animals.

"*Buenos dias*," greeted Guadalupe.

"The day is good enough," replied Gonzales gruffly, as he flung his reins to the waiting Felipe and strode up to the doorway.

"Get us food and drink," he ordered.

His wide shoulders brushed the sides of the doorway as he entered.

"Food and drink you shall have," grinned Guadalupe. "You come at a good time, Gonzales."

"Any time is good," replied Gonzales, catching sight of Torres.

He chuckled deeply in his throat and tossed his hat to the table.

"*Tequila*," he grunted. "*Tequila* first and then food. Good day, Torres."

"Good day," said Torres unevenly.

169

There was little friendship between them. Lopez entered, bearing several bottles of the white liquor, and placed them on Gonzales' table, together with some empty cups.

Gonzales smashed the neck from a bottle across the edge of a table and poured a cupful.

"Come and drink, Torres," he ordered.

Torres came to the table and accepted a cup. He knew it would not be well to refuse Gonzales.

"What is the news!" asked Gonzales, turning to Guadalupe.

"News is never plentiful at the Rancho Sierra," replied the old Mexican. "But you come in time for our little *fiesta*. Felipe leaves at once for Santa Isabella to fetch a priest."

"*Madre de Dios!*" swore Gonzales. "And why a priest, old man? Is it that someone is dying?"

Guadalupe laughed and shook his head.

"A priest for the wedding of our Torres, Gonzales."

Gonzales threw back his head and started at Torres, stroking his black mustaches violently.

"For the wedding of Torres, eh? Ho, ho, ho, ho! A *fiesta* for the wedding of Torres at Rancho Sierra! Now and then he must have his little joke. And who would marry Torres?"

Torres squirmed in his chair. He was less drunk now.

"And why not?" he demanded. "Have I not the right, Gonzales?"

"My question is not answered," reminded Gonzales. "Does he marry some flat-faced daughter of a peon, or a dancing girl from the dives of the south?"

170

"A gringo bride," laughed Guadalupe. "She came to him across a saddle, roped, that she might not fail to be here at the wedding. And" — Guadalupe laughed softly, silently — "oh another horse came the mother, also roped. Have you a musician, Gonzales?"

Gonzales roared with laughter and opened another bottle, while Torres scowled heavily and fingered the knife in his sleeve.

"A musician?" queried Gonzales, after he recovered from his fit of merriment. "I have Manuelo, who is never far from his beloved guitar. But that is of little importance. Where is the bride?"

Torres scowled and helped himself to another drink, while Guadalupe waited for him to speak. Gonzales grew impatient.

"Have you hidden her away where she may not look upon men?" he demanded. "Let us see if she is worthy of you, *ladron*."

"She is worthy of any man," grunted Torres. "Let us drink and forget the women."

But Gonzales was not to be put off. He surged to his feet and flung a broken-necked bottle at Guadalupe's head. Fortunately for Guadalupe, Gonzales' aim was very poor.

"Bring her out, Guadalupe," he ordered. "Hell, do I have to make my request more plain?"

Torres slumped in his chair, glowering at the bottles, while Guadalupe shuffled to the end of the room against the bluff, where he drew aside a cowhide-covered bunk, which concealed a trap door. Flinging this back he disappeared down a short flight of stairs.

171

Gonzales drank gulpingly and laughed at Torres, "So, you stole a gringo girl, eh?" he mocked. "Fool! When you go back across the line they will cut off your ears."

"Who spoke of going back?" demanded Torres. "The world is wide. Anyway" — Torres shrugged his shoulders — "what is one girl, more or less?"

Gonzales' two men came in and he motioned them to sit down at another table. Garcia came in, his scowling face half-concealed in the dirty serape, and sat down against the wall.

Gonzales tossed a bottle of *tequila* across to his men, who thanked him profusely and proceeded to empty it. Voices came from within the trap door, and a moment later Wanna Hawkworth came slowly up the ladder, closely followed by Guadalupe.

The girl was not bound now. Her wealth of blue-black hair hung in profusion about her face, which was slightly pale. Her calico dress had been badly torn, but she never looked more beautiful than standing there at the edge of the trap door, her hands clenched at her sides, staring her hate at Torres.

Gonzales half-rose from his chair as he stared at her. He had expected nothing like this. Torres reached for another bottle.

With a mighty oath, Gonzales attempted to bow and almost struck his forehead on the table. He shoved it roughly aside and went toward Wanna, who backed away.

"Let her alone," ordered Guadalupe. "She belongs to Torres."

Gonzales stopped and leered at Guadalupe.

172

"Belongs to Torres!" he roared. "To that?" He pointed at Torres, who was shakily pouring a drink. "*Dios!* Here is a mate for a man!"

But Gonzales did not advance farther. He seemed content for the moment merely to look at her. It was Lopez who broke the spell, as he shuffled quickly in from the kitchen.

"*Vaqueros!*" he said shrilly, pointing toward the north. "*Americanos!*"

"*Diablo!*" swore Guadalupe. "Who can this be?"

He grasped Wanna by the arm, whirled her around, and hurried her down the ladder, while Gonzales turned and walked drunkenly back toward the doorway, passing Torres, who had slumped at the word *Americanos*. He was too drunk to flee, and he felt sure, deep in his crooked soul, that retribution had overtaken him.

CHAPTER
FOURTEEN

"MY FRIEND HAS A CHILL"

Gonzales leaned in the doorway and watched the riders draw up in the yard. Baldy Kern was in the lead, and behind him came Baum, Kohler, Horan, Doctor Meline and his son. Strapped to the back of the gray horse was Hashknife Hartley, bound tightly and blind-folded. "Hello, *compadre*," called Gonzales, as he recognized Baldy.

"Hyah, Gonzales," laughed Baldy. "How yuh comin'?"

Another horseman came into view. It was Lee Yung. He was not much of a rider, which accounted for his slower pace. They dismounted as Guadalupe came out past Gonzales and greeted them. Lee Yung and Guadalupe were old friends, and the Chinaman spoke Spanish fluently.

"What of the prisoner?" asked Guadalupe in Spanish.

And while the rest of the cavalcade listened with little understanding, Lee Yung told Guadalupe why they had taken Hashknife prisoner. It took some little time.

"And will bringing him here give you back the stuff?" asked Guadalupe.

"Perhaps," replied Lee Yung. "There are ways of making men talk. This man knows where it is hidden. The big man over there is Doctor Meline, who disposes of what we get. The young man is his son."

"It is good," nodded Guadalupe. "Go inside."

Baldy, Kohler, and Horan took the ropes off Hashknife and slid him from the saddle. He was unable to stand, unable to see through the heavy bandage; so they half-carried, half-dragged him into the house and propped him up in a chair.

His hat was gone, and the welt on his head showed plainly. But not a sound issued from his lips, although he was suffering tortures from returning circulation. His wrists were blue and swollen from the tight ropes, and his limbs twitched from the reaction.

"By God, he's got nerve!" exclaimed Jack Meline admiringly.

"We'll break that," declared his father.

Baldy had caught sight of Torres, who had not moved from the table. Garcia still sat against the wall, paying no attention to the newcomers.

"So this is where you hold out, eh?" snarled Baldy. "I've been lookin' for yuh, Torres."

Baldy went closer to him, his hand resting on the butt of his gun, but Guadalupe, sensing the danger, stepped between them.

"Not here," he told Baldy in English. "This is no place to even scores. At this *rancho*, everybody is a friend. It must be that way or no one is safe."

Baldy glowered at Guadalupe for a moment, but could see the wisdom of Guadalupe's words.

"All right," he growled. "I'll catch him away from here."

"*Esta buena*," nodded Guadalupe. "But not here, *compadre*."

"How's chances to get somethin' to eat?" asked Kohler.

Guadalupe nodded and went into the kitchen to give Lopez his orders, after which he went outside, shuffled around to the corral, where he instructed Felipe about going to Santa Isabella.

Baldy examined Hashknife's ropes and removed the cloth from around his eyes.

"It won't hurt yuh none to have a look now," he grinned. "You ain't in a place where yore eyes will do yuh much good."

Hashknife blinked painfully, but said nothing. The bandage had been over his eyes since before he had regained consciousness, and the light hurt them. He shut his eyes until the stinging sensation had somewhat passed, and then looked around.

He had heard enough during the trip to know who his captors were and what they had in store for him. Gonzales swaggered over in front of him and grinned widely.

"You like drink some *tequila?*" he asked.

Hashknife had not been long enough in the border country to know the meaning of *tequila*. Gonzales strode back to a table, poured a drink into a tin cup, and held it to Hashknife's lips.

"What in hell do you want to waste good liquor for?" demanded Kohler angrily.

176

Hashknife gulped the big drink and thanked Gonzales with a look. Gonzales turned and scowled at Kohler.

"I pay for this *tequila*," he told Kohler. "And what I pay for I use as I like, *hombre*."

"Sure, sure!" interposed Baldy. "That's all right, Gonzales."

Gonzales drank and walked outside, where he ran into Guadalupe.

"I have just sent Felipe to Santa Isabella," said Guadalupe.

"That is good," agreed Gonzales. "But other things are not good. Torres stole this girl from Hawk Hole; these men are from Hawk Hole. There is bad blood between Torres and Kern. If they learn that these women are concealed here, it may not be good for us."

"They could gain nothing by spoiling our schemes, Gonzales."

Gonzales laughed softly and shook his head.

"Never trust a gringo," he advised. "When their own color is concerned, they do not always count the cost. In many ways they are very great fools."

"They will go back before the priest comes."

"We do not know," argued Gonzales. "They have said that this tall prisoner's friend escaped to carry the news, and Hawk Hole will be a dangerous place for them. They will torture the tall one, in order to force him to confess, but what then? By this time there are men riding toward the border, Guadalupe, my friend."

"What would you do?" asked Guadalupe anxiously.

"Ah!"

Gonzales stroked his mustaches and looked very wise.

"Torres is drunk," he declared. "The girl is worth too much to become the bride of Torres. Suppose we remove the girl in the night, my friend. By morning —"

"You would take her from Torres?"

"I have seen her," said Gonzales meaningly.

But Guadalupe shook his head quickly.

"It is a matter between you and Torres. Steve Guadalupe plays fair with all. No man can ever say that he lost by trusting me. What men do between themselves is nothing to me, but I have nothing to look back at and fear. Torres brought the girl to me, and he offers one hundred dollars in American gold for the use of a priest. I have agreed. That is my answer, Gonzales."

Gonzales tugged at his mustaches. He knew that Guadalupe would not be a party to his scheme, because it would be a case of discriminating against one of his guests.

"Suppose we leave it to the girl," he suggested.

Guadalupe laughed and shrugged his shoulders.

"Very well. And suppose she refuses either? What then?"

Gonzales patted himself on the chest and smiled widely. He was egotistical enough to think that any woman would be attracted to him, when as a matter of fact, Wanna would probably select Torres, as being the lesser of the two evils.

Guadalupe went back to the kitchen to hurry Lopez, and Gonzales entered the house. Torres had fallen forward against the table, his face buried in his arms —

178

dead drunk. The men from the K-10 were grouped together, talking in undertones. Hashknife sat where they had left him, tightly bound, staring out through the open door. He had spoken no word since Kohler's rifle barrel had laid him low.

Baldy left the group and came to him. Hashknife lifted his eyes and squinted at the boss of the K-10.

"Ready to talk?" asked Baldy.

"About what?" asked Hashknife weakly.

"You know damn well what about. We want to know what yuh clone with the cargo of drugs and you'll tell us, *sabe?*"

"Will I?" Hashknife smiled, but shook his head.

"Oh, yeah, yuh will," persisted Baldy. "We're in Mexico now in a safe place. We know how to make yuh talk, Hartley, and it'll save yuh a lot of hell, if you'll speak up now."

"If yuh knew, yuh wouldn't dare go after it," said Hashknife easily. "I heard enough to know that my pardner got away, and he'll sure make life miserable for you women stealers."

"Women stealers?" asked Baldy wonderingly. "What do yuh mean?"

"I reckon you know, Kern. You go back across the line and see how quick yuh get hung."

The rest of the K-10 gang moved in closer, wondering what Hashknife meant. Torres lifted his head slightly, a drunken grin on his lips. Gonzales scowled. He did not want that outfit to know about the girl.

"What women are you talking about?" demanded Doctor Meline.

"Big Medicine Hawkworth's wife and daughter."

"Well, what about 'em?" snapped Baldy.

"You ought to know, Kern. You helped search the Tumbling H ranch-house and kidnap the women."

"That's a damn lie!"

"Oh, all right."

Hashknife shut his lips tightly.

"Let's get this straight," said Jack Meline, crowding in closer. "You say that Mrs. Hawkworth and Wanna have been taken away, Hartley?"

"Who done it?" asked Baldy. "By God, we didn't!"

Hashknife knew that they were telling the truth. In fact, he doubted that they had from the first, but wanted to be sure.

When Hashknife refused to talk any more, Baldy's eyes fastened on Torres, and he walked over to the hunched figure.

"Where's the woman and girl, Torres?" he asked.

"*Quien sabe?*" grunted Torres. "I know nothing about women."

"Why all this talk about women and girls?" asked Gonzales. "Are they your friends, Kern?"

"They are not," denied Kern. "I don't care a damn who took 'em, but I don't want the blame."

"You'll have a mighty short time to protest yore innocence; if yuh go back across the border," said Hashknife.

"Aw, shut up!" snarled Baldy. "Damn yuh, you won't live to enjoy it, anyway."

"Mebbe not," Hashknife smiled softly. "Yuh never can tell. I'll die when my time comes and not before,

180

Kern. Yore mistake was in lettin' my pardner get away. The Tumblin H outfit were waitin' in Pinnacle for him, and I'm bettin' that most of the town is with 'em now."

"You fool!" snarled Kohler. "This is Mexico. They won't dare cross the line."

"You crossed it, didn't yuh?"

"Well, we —" Kohler floundered.

"Would Big Medicine care about the border?" asked Hashknife.

Doctor Meline swore viciously and turned away. Lopez was coming in with dishes of food and placing them on a long table.

Baldy walked over and sat down at the table. Meline followed and sat down beside Baldy.

"There's a lot of truth in what he says," declared the doctor. "We have made a serious mistake, Baldy. For the price of one cargo we have jeopardized our future. We can't afford to be found here."

"Well, hell, we can't go back."

"I can at least," said the doctor nervously. "No one knows that I am with you, that I ever came to Hawk Hole."

"Gettin' cold feet, eh?" sneered Baldy. "Hey! Steve! Bring us some *tequila*. My friend has a chill. C'mon and set down, the rest of yuh. What the hell are yuh all lookin' so blue about? By God, I didn't know I was workin' with a lot of sheep."

"I'm not afraid," declared Jack Meline, "but I'd give quite a lot to be out of this damn country and on my way back to Frisco. It surely don't look good to me."

181

"Soak up some *tequila* and the world will look brighter."

Guadalupe was generous with his liquor, and they attacked it with a will. *Tequila* is potent liquor, and its full effect comes suddenly. Gonzales sat at the far end of the room, drinking alone, thinking deeply. His two men remained outside, each of them half-asleep. Torres still appeared to sleep at the table, while Garcia still squatted against the wall, half-covered with his serape.

The *tequila* seemed to have the desired effect, and those at the long table became jovial. Even Doctor Meline forgot his fears and matched drinks with the rest of the crowd. Guadalupe sat down with them and helped drink some of his own liquor.

The liquor gave them prodigious appetites and they did justice to the simple and none too clean cooking of Lopez. No one offered Hashknife food nor drink and he asked for none.

It was growing dark now, and Lopez brought in a lighted lamp for the center of the table.

"How about stickin' a guard down the trail?" asked Baldy. "We don't want somebody runnin' in on us, Steve."

"I have none," said Guadalupe. "Felipe is gone. Perhaps I might have Lopez watch the trail."

"I send my two men," offered Gonzales, and went out to them.

"That'll make me set easier," declared Baldy. "Let's have a few more bottles, Steve. I feel like a bird tonight."

"And we have some work to do presently," said Meline, nodding toward Hashknife. "But that can wait."

CHAPTER
FIFTEEN

SLEEPY FINDS HIMSELF IN A HOLE

Sleepy and the men from the Tumbling H rode back to Pinnacle with the intention of enlisting the assistance of the sheriff and deputy. They realized that their force was too small for an invasion of Mexico.

But they found Cloudy Day leaning against the Greenback bar, singing a mournful song, and too drunk to be of any use. Lon Pelly was in a poker game, also very drunk, but with all the appearance of a sober man. He left the game at Sleepy's request, and went outside while they told him what they intended to do.

They only told him that they needed his help in going to the Rancho Sierra to find some folks who had been kidnapped, but Lon was too drunk to take an interest in the matter.

"Aw, let the damn fool go back to his game!" grunted Ike. "He's only good for poker-playin'."

Lon took no offense, but went back to his game.

"What did they want, Lon?" asked Faro Lanning.

"They're all crazy," declared Lon owlishly. "They want me to go to the Rancho Sierra to whip Mexico. Nawshir, not me. Whose deal?"

"Your deal," said Faro, turning and motioning to Arkansas Jones, who was standing at the bar.

Faro got up and told Arkansas to take charge of the game. "I'm goin' to eat," he said.

He hurried out through the rear door, went out to his stable, where he saddled a horse and rode away. Judging from appearances, Faro Lanning was going quite a way to get a meal.

Sleepy and Big Medicine went to a store and purchased some rifle cartridges, while Ike Musical, and Cleve procured a few articles of food, which might be carried in their pockets or tied to a saddle.

They rode out of Pinnacle, as if heading for the Tumbling H, but changed their course toward the south as soon as they left the town. Big Medicine had not complained over his loss, but there was an expression in his eyes which boded no good to the guilty parties.

They crossed the divide and followed the old road to the border, where they struck the trail to the Rancho Sierra. There were plenty of horse tracks in the dusty trail, all pointing to the south.

"Plenty horses goin' in," observed Sleepy. "And we've got to be danged observin', gents. I understand that these folks down here get kinda careless when it comes to foolin' with another man's life."

"And I'm one of 'em, if I find the jigger that broke my phonygraft record," declared Musical. "That's what yuh might call bein' rowdyish, ain't it?"

"Aw, yuh can get another record," growled Ike.

"Thasso? Not just like that, Ike. That singer's dead now."

"I'd 'a' bet on that," said Cleve. "No danged human could sing thataway and live."

Musical grumbled to himself something about some folks not having an ear for music, but finally dropped the subject. The trail wound in and out of the rocky, brush-covered hills, where an army could hide.

Ike had ridden almost to the ranch one day, looking for stolen cattle, and had viewed the place from a rocky point, so he was elected to guide the party to this place.

After considerable loss of time Ike finally discovered the place where he had left the trail, and they managed to reach the eminence, which was about half a mile from the ranch. They crouched in the brush and watched the ranch, but at that distance they were unable to distinguish individuals.

"Must be at least twenty horses in that corral," observed Sleepy. "If there's a man for every horse, we've got some gang to bust into."

"And a very bad place to attack," declared Big Medicine.

"Shore is," agreed Musical. "Looks like our best bet was to make our big move after dark."

Sleepy had been studying the place for several minutes, while the others discussed a possible point of attack.

"It's a risky business to butt right into that place," declared Sleepy. "We don't know a danged thing about who is there, nor what we're goin' up against. See that butte back of the house? That's where I'm goin'. I'll circle back and manage to work my way over that butte, *sabe?*

"That'll let me down pretty darned close. Mebbe I can get on their roof. Anyway, I'll scheme some way to find out what's inside that place. They won't look for anybody to come in on 'em from that side. You stay here, where yuh can see me work my way down the bluff. If nothin' happens I'll go back the same way."

"Suppose somethin' happens?" questioned Musical.

"Then it happens," grinned Sleepy. "If I don't come back, you can come ahead, but don't do it in daylight."

"All right, Stevens." Big Medicine held out his hand. "Good luck to you. If we hear any shooting, we won't wait for darkness."

"All right."

Sleepy slipped off his cartridge belt, containing rifle cartridges, and handed it to Musical, who also took charge of Sleepy's rifle. He intended to travel light.

It did not take Sleepy long to find that it was impossible to use his horse, unless he was equipped to cut a trail through the brush, so he left the animal with the others and went on. By a dint of maneuvering he was able to work his way across the hills, in and out of narrow cañons, where the mesquite threatened to make rags of all of his clothes.

It took him at least an hour to gain the foot of the tall bluff, and another hour to reach the top. He was thoroughly tired out and bleeding from innumerable scratches. The ranch-house was not visible, nor could he determine just which pinnacle the gang were

186

inhabiting, so he waved his hat wildly several times, hoping that they would catch his signal.

Then he began the descent. He was about to remove his boots, thinking that it might lessen the sound of his approach, but a big rattler buzzed at him from a rubble of rocks, and he voted to keep his boots where they belonged.

Darkness follows the sunset quickly in the border country; there is no twilight worthy of the name, and the sun had set. Sleepy knew that he was getting well down the bluff, and that it behooved him to go softly. A dislodged stone would probably roll all the way to the ranch-house, so Sleepy peered closely before placing his heels.

It was very brushy; dry brush, which crackled at the touch. And the light was failing very fast. Already the darkness had blotted out the pinnacle beyond.

Sleepy felt that he was near the edge of the bluff. He could smell the odors of cooking and of wood smoke. He eased his foot through a tangle of brush, tested the ground, and swung his body forward.

As he brought his two feet together, something seemed to jerk the ground from under his feet and he shot downward into a hole. He seemed to be falling down an incline, fairly going end over end, the bottom of the fall ending in a blaze of glory, in which Sleepy lost all interest in things.

But just a few minutes before the Tumbling H men had reached the lookout point, Faro Lanning had ridden up to the Rancho Sierra. He had been passed by the guards, who knew him, and had told them to keep a good watch.

And he had walked into the ranch-house only to find the K-10 gang making merry over their meal.

"What in hell are you doin' down here?" demanded Baldy.

"Riding around," said Lanning uneasily. "Where's Torres?"

One of the men indicated Torres, asleep on the table. Lanning shook him, but Torres merely grunted and continued to snore.

"C'mon and have drink," invited Kohler. "What the hell, we're all good fellers together."

"All right."

Lanning realized that they were all half-drunk. He accepted a bottle and cup and sat down at the table.

"This is all right," said Baldy seriously, "but what are you doin' here, Faro? What's the idea?"

"I might ask the same question, if I was curious."

"Well, I am curious, Faro."

"All right."

Faro drained his cup and threw it back on the table.

"You might like to know that Big Medicine and his gang are comin' here. I heard 'em say they were. They tried to get Lon Pelly to come with 'em, but Lon was too drunk. I had a hunch that some of my friends might like to know it."

"*Esta buena!*" grunted Guadalupe. "We will welcome 'em, eh?"

"Damn right!" chuckled Kohler. "Whatcha say, Gonzales?"

188

"We will show them the good time, *compadre*."

"I saw the guards," offered Faro. "I warned 'em."

Faro saw Hashknife, and a grin wreathed his lips.

"He won't be much help to Hawkworth," laughed Baldy.

Hashknife did not speak to Faro, and the gang went back to their drinking. Lee Yung drank little. He considered Faro Lanning thoughtfully, distrustfully. He knew that Faro had some real reason for riding down there. And he had asked for Torres.

In spite of his dangerous predicament Hashknife smiled to himself. It was evident that there were two factions, composed of the K-10 outfit on one side and Torres and Lanning on the other. He wondered who else was connected with Torres' side.

He knew now that Jack Hill was Jack Meline, and that the elder Meline was closely associated with both Lee Yung and Baldy Kern. He wondered what Sleepy and the Tumbling H gang were doing, and from the talk he had heard he knew that the K-10 outfit had nothing to do with the kidnapping of Lucy and Wanna. He was also beginning to fear that Big Medicine was wrong in thinking that the women had been taken to this ranch.

Hashknife noted with satisfaction that everyone was drinking considerable liquor. Given enough time, he was sure that Sleepy and the gang would make a desperate attempt to find him. But Baldy was hardly satisfied with Faro Lanning's explanation of his appearance. Baldy was just drunk enough to be suspicious.

"You must 'a' hurried, Faro," he observed.

"I didn't lose much time," agreed Faro indifferently.

"How did yuh know yuh had friends here?"

"Guessed it."

Faro winked wisely.

"What made Big Medicine think we came here?"

"I dunno. Pass me that bottle, will yuh, Kohler? I never asked Big Medicine 'cause I didn't talk to him. Lon told me."

"Uh-huh." Baldy glowered drunkenly. "And why did you ask for Torres?"

"I — I dunno," Faro faltered. "Mebbe Lon mentioned Torres."

"Very likely."

"We're all friends together," mumbled Kohler. "Whatsa use of quarrelin'? Steve, my bottle is empty."

"Just like yore head," grumbled Baldy. "We're in a hell of a fix, if yuh ask me. That damned outfit knows that we came here."

"What if they do?" Thus Horan boastingly. "We're here first."

"I have my men watching," stated Gonzales easily.

"Yeah — fine. They was half-drunk when we came. Hell, a railroad tram could pass them two jiggers."

Baldy got up from the table and went unsteadily to the door, giving Hashknife a nasty look as he passed. The others laughed at Baldy's fears, while Guadalupe brought more liquor.

It was light enough for Baldy to distinguish objects at a distance, and as he leaned against the side of the

190

door, two riders came around the corner of the house and drew up near the door.

One was Felipe, the half-wit, and the other was unmistakably a priest. Baldy whirled, shut the door, and called to Guadalupe:

"Steve, who in hell sent for a priest?"

"*Diablo!*" exploded Guadalupe. "I did not expect him so soon. Quick! Take your prisoner!"

Guadalupe ran to the corner, swung the old bunk aside, and lifted the trap, while Baldy and Gonzales picked Hashknife up bodily and hurried him the length of the room. His legs were bound so he could not walk, and they lowered him swiftly to Guadalupe, after which Gonzales helped him below.

It was only a matter of a few moments before Guadalupe and Gonzales came back, closed the trap, and were ready when Felipe opened the door and admitted the priest.

The priest was a small man, with a thin face, almost chalklike in color. He halted just inside the door and surveyed the company.

"I am Father Francisco," he announced in a monotone. "Felipe met me on the road, so I saved him the trip to Santa Isabella. He said that you had need of my services."

"Welcome, Father," said Guadalupe. "I shall have Lopez bring food and wine at once."

"Thank you, son," replied the priest.

Baldy laughed aloud. It amused him to have a priest, at least twenty years younger than Guadalupe, call him son. "They sent for yuh, did they?" asked Baldy, addressing the priest.

"So I believe."

"Uh-huh."

Baldy squinted narrowly at Guadalupe, who turned toward the kitchen.

"Say, Stevie," he said thickly, "what's the idea of this priest comin' here? Who sent for him?"

Guadalupe hesitated for a moment before pointing at Gonzales.

"Ask Gonzales."

"*Buena,*" laughed Gonzales, "I can tell you. It is to marry Gonzales that the priest comes, my friend."

"You lie!" Torres straightened up, seemingly sober and glared at Gonzales. "You lie, you *ladron!*"

Gonzales almost fell down in starting toward Torres, but Baldy blocked him.

"Hang on to yourself," advised Baldy.

"Torres you set down, before I come over there and knock yuh down. Now" — he shook the massive Gonzales — "tell me about it. Let Torres alone, I tell yuh!"

"She is my woman," declared Torres. "I brought her here. That pig of a *contrabandista* would steal her from me."

"Thish is gettin' good," declared Kohler drunkenly, while the rest of his companions agreed that it was worth listening to.

"You brought her, eh?" grunted Baldy. "How about it, Gonzales?"

192

"I do not deny it. But he is not a man. This woman is fit to mate with a man, with me!"

"Egotist!" spat Lee Yung.

"Where is this woman?" demanded Baldy. "Who is she?"

"She is the daughter of Hawkworth," said Torres.

He did not want them to know this, but there was no way out of it.

"Hawkworth's daughter! So you stole her, eh? You poor fool! If I was Hawkworth I'd flay you and use your hide for a saddle cover. But where is she?"

"Who knows?" laughed Gonzales. "She will be here at the wedding."

"At my wedding," corrected Torres. "I demand that I have the right to marry her. Didn't I bring both of them here?"

"Both of 'em?" wondered Baldy. "F'r God's sake, what's the idea of bringin' two?"

"Her mother came also."

Baldy threw back his head and laughed loudly.

"Well, he started in right, boys; he took mamma along. Now the question is who will marry her? What'll yuh do, draw straws or roll the dice? Yuh can't fight it out. Torres is too small."

"A knife makes us even, *senor*," said Torres stiffly.

"And she'd sure have a bloody bridegroom," declared Horan. "I've seen the finish of a few knife fights. Why not leave it to the *padre?*"

"That's the stuff," agreed Baldy. "You pick the winner, old priest. Look 'em over and see which one would make the best husband for a girl."

"Not without an understanding," said the priest. "What was meant by saying that the girl was, stolen?"

"Aw, that was a joke," said Kohler. "Everythin' is all right. Father Francisco."

"But has the girl no choice in the matter?"

"Well," laughed Baldy, "it kinda looks like Torres was goin' to marry her, until along comes Gonzales and smears things. If the girl wants Torres, she'll have Torres, I reckon. Hey! Steve! Bring out the bride. We'll find out who she wants."

Guadalupe opened the trap and went down the short flight of stairs, while they opened more liquor and joked about the coming nuptials. The priest looked on gravely, wondering what he should do under the circumstances.

Lucy, the old squaw, was first up the ladder, followed closely by Wanna. Guadalupe came up behind them, but did not close the trap. Jack Meline started toward them, but his father drew him back.

"Oh, this is a rotten deal!" declared Jack hotly.

He was not so drunk that he did not realize what it meant.

"You keep out of it!" snapped the elder Meline. "It is none of your affair."

Neither of the women spoke. Lucy seemed at the verge of exhaustion, but Wanna looked at them defiantly. Her eyes rested on Jack Meline's face and she gave a start.

"You here?" she said dully.

"Yes, I'm here," he replied.

"And you keep your beak out of it," warned Baldy. "We don't need yore help."

He turned to Wanna and looked her over appraisingly.

"So yo're Big Medicine's girl, eh? Not such a bad looker, at that. What we want to know is this" — indicating Gonzales and Torres, with a sweep of his hand — "which one do yuh want?"

Wanna looked wonderingly at the two men, and shook her head.

"I don't know what you mean," she said slowly.

"Don'tcha? Well, both of 'em want to marry yuh. Which one do yuh chose? It don't make a damn bit of difference to us. Pick yore man and we'll see that the other keeps out. The priest is ready and the goose hangs high."

"Neither," said Wanna defiantly.

Baldy laughed at Gonzales and Torres.

"That's another angle," he chuckled. "It seems that the lady don't care for either of yuh. Well I don't blame her a damn bit."

"We do not ask you to decide," reminded Torres. "This marriage has nothing to do with you, Kern."

"Thasso?" Baldy laughed. "Keep yore shirt on, Torres. There's goin' to be a marriage, and yuh can bet on that."

"There's several of us here," laughed Kohler. "Why marry her off to either one of the *colorado maduros*, when there's good white men to be had for the askin'?"

"Wanna" — it was Jack Meline — "will you marry me?"

195

His answer came in a back-handed slap from his father, and he went back against the wall, bleeding at the mouth.

"Keep out of this, you fool!" roared Meline.

He was half-drunk, and caught at the corner of the table to keep his balance. Jack wiped the blood from his lips, but said nothing. He had tried to do what he considered the decent thing, as long as they intended to force marriage upon her.

"Let's pull off a raffle," suggested Kohler. "The lucky man marries the girl. How's that for an idea?"

But before Baldy could digest the idea, one of the guards fairly fell in through the doorway, with the other close behind.

"They come!" panted one of the guards. "Four riders."

"How close?" demanded Gonzales anxiously.

"Not too far. It is better to get them here than to fight in the dark. They will soon be here, because the house seems dark."

"Big Medicine and his gang!" exploded Baldy. "We'll trap 'em. Take the women into the kichen. Leave the lamp as it is. Scatter and lie down on the floor, but keep yore guns ready. By God, we've got 'em, boys! Make it fast."

CHAPTER
SIXTEEN

DRESSED TO KILL

Guadalupe and Felipe hurried the two women into the kitchen and barred the door leading to the outside, while the others, except the priest, flung themselves on the floor, away from the rays of the lamp, and covered the doorway with their guns. The priest moved toward the door, but was stopped by Baldy.

"Get back by the table!" snapped Baldy. "I ain't never killed no priests, but there's always a first time."

Father Francisco moved back to the table, where he stood full in the rays of the lamp, looking toward the doorway. The place was as silent at the tomb, except for the breathing of the men.

It seemed ages before there was any sound from outside. Came the soft crunch of gravel and the door was flung violently open. Still there was no one in sight. The door creaked back a trifle. Then Big Medicine Hawkworth's huge body filled the doorway, a heavy revolver in his right hand. He squinted at the light and at the black-gowned priest, blinking slightly.

"Only a priest," he said softly. "That's queer."

He stepped inside, followed by Ike Marsh, Musical Matthews, and Cleve Davis.

"A priest, eh?" said Ike nervously.

"Don't move." Baldy's voice was triumphant. "There's a dozen guns on yuh right now. Put up yore hands and drop them guns."

The capture was a complete success. They realized that it was useless to resist. The men were scattered along the wall, and now the men from the Tumbling H could distinguish them and their guns.

Kohler came and collected the guns from the floor, handing them to Guadalupe for safe keeping, while the rest of the men got up and came forward. Big Medicine leaned back against the wall and looked at the well-known faces.

"Thought you'd catch us asleep, eh?" sneered Baldy. "We've been expectin' yuh."

Baldy looked them over curiously.

"Where's that damn Stevens?" he asked suddenly.

Ike Marsh laughed with relief. He was afraid that they had already captured Sleepy, who had not come back to them. Baldy scowled and repeated his question.

"Yuh might do a little guessin'," said Ike. "We always have an ace in the hole, Kern."

"Thasso? Well, yore aces won't help yuh none this time, Marsh. We've got the whole deck ag'in yore one."

Doctor Meline had come into the lamplight, and Big Medicine was staring at him, an amazed expression on his face. He moved toward Meline, unheeding the menace of several guns.

"Hey!" snapped Baldy. "Get back there, Hawkworth!"

But Hawkworth did not seem to hear Baldy's warning. Meline stepped back and put the table between himself and Big Medicine.

"You," said Big Medicine hoarsely. "What are you doing here?"

Doctor Meline laughed nervously.

"Man, can't you talk?" demanded Big Medicine.

"Oh, I can talk all right," said Meline.

"Then go ahead. I don't understand it."

Big Medicine swung his head and looked at the crown, but his gaze came back to Meline.

"You are Doctor Meline?"

It was both a question and a statement.

"The notorious Doctor Meline," corrected Torres. "The biggest drug-seller in the West, the crook who sent you a bundle of paper instead of money."

Big Medicine stared at Torres. Meline whirled angrily on the Mexican, but decided that it was better to face on man at a time.

"Is this true, Jim Meline?" asked Big Medicine hoarsely.

"True?" Meline laughed. "Well, if it is — what then?"

Big Medicine's right hand went to his face and he drew the back of his hand across his mouth. The lines of his face seemed to deepen.

"I trusted you, Jim," he said simply.

"You always was a fool," declared Meline. "I might as well spill it all now, Hawkworth. The money you sent me for the past twenty-odd years had been well spent. It has bought me many things.

"You fool, you buried yourself down here in the hills, and gave me your money to invest. Oh, I've invested it well" — Meline laughed recklessly. "I'll admit that I got quite a shock when you sent for twenty thousand dollars.

"But I sent it to you, a whole package of bogus money, and some damn fool held up the stage and stole it. Ha, ha, ha ha! I intended for the stage to be robbed, but by a different outfit. The package was to come back to me intact, so that none would ever know what it contained."

"You did this, Jim?" Big Medicine spoke softly, sorrowfully. "We were friends once, Jim. I would have backed you with my life. In all the wide world there was no man I trusted as I did you, and you do this thing to me."

Big Medicine shook his head slowly, his lips compressed.

"I can't believe it yet, Jim. I feel that I will awake after a while and find that it is only a dream. Jim Meline, the one man I thought I could trust."

He shifted his eyes and caught sight of Jack's pale face with the smear of blood across his lips.

"You are all here," he said slowly. "Lee Yung, Torres, Jack Hill — well, what is the program? What is this priest doing here?"

Baldy laughed mockingly.

"Put four chairs against the wall and set down our guests," he ordered. "Kohler, you and Baum set over here and keep yore guns on 'em, sabe? Guadalupe, you bring in the bride. By God, we'll have a marriage, if I have to be the bridegroom myself."

200

Baldy turned angrily to Doctor Meline.

"So yore money package was a dummy, eh? You didn't trust us to send it back, didja Meline? And all yore yelpin' about losin' twenty thousand dollars was only a lie! You sent that fool kid in to take it back to you."

"What is that to you?" demanded Meline hotly.

"Nothin', only yore crooked work has put us in danged bad. You ain't got no more sense than to write letters that anybody might steal."

"My crooked work?" Meline laughed. "You've got a lot of nerve to yelp about crooked work."

"I never played crooked with my own kind," retorted Baldy.

The boys began arranging the four chairs against the wall, while Guadalupe went to the kitchen, carrying the cap tired weapons, which he placed on the kitchen table. Felipe and Lopez had been guarding the women but now Guadalupe signalled them to precede him into the other room.

Felipe and Lopez grinned at each other, as they drank from a jug. "There is not much left," informed Lopez, shaking the jug.

"Then hide it," said Felipe, who was a half-wit.

Lopez unbarred the kitchen door and placed the jug outside, after which he shut the door and went into the other room.

Sleepy had no idea of where he was nor how long he had been there when he awoke in the dark. His head was splitting and he felt that most of his body had been hammered to a pulp. He had a painful scalp wound, which he examined with his fingertips, and one of his eyes was almost swelled shut.

Investigation showed that in spite of his fall, his sixshooter was still in its holster. For several minutes he lay quiet, trying to remember just what had happened to him.

"Fell's into a damned old prospect hole, I suppose," he told himself disgustedly.

But it was a big prospect hole, he decided, after trying to reach the walls. Twisting his gaze upward he got a glimpse of the sky, a starry circle some distance above him.

"That's where I came from," he told himself. "I sure done a regular Santa Claus down that damned chimney. I hope to gosh I ain't broke nothin'."

He flexed his legs and arms, which pained him considerably, but he was soon assured that no bones were broken. Moving in directly under the opening he found a ladder, which extended upward. He laughed painfully and rubbed his nose. From somewhere he could hear the soft drone of voices.

He listened closely. They did not seem to come from above. He was unable to distinguish what was being said, but was very sure that it was a number of people talking.

Cautiously he moved along away from the ladder. It seemed to be a sort of cave, rather than a prospect hole. He bumped into a projection and almost fell. Around this projection and about thirty feet away he could see the faint glow of a light. It was from the room above the trap door, but Sleepy had no way of knowing this.

He moved slowly toward this faint illumination and tripped over some object, sprawling on his hands and knees. He swore softly, as his sore hands and knees came in contact with the ground.

"Sleepy!" a voice whispered.

Sleepy sat up, rubbing his knees.

"Is that you, Hashknife?" he asked softly.

He did not seem to be surprised.

"Yeah, it's me. Got a knife?"

"I s'pose so. Got yuh tied up, pardner?"

Sleepy took out his pocket-knife and in a few moments Hashknife was free. His hands were swollen from the tight ropes, and his arms seemed little better than clubs, but he knew they would soon be all right again.

"What's that ahead of us?" whispered Sleepy.

"Trap door into the ranch-house," replied Hashknife painfully rubbing his wrists. "How in hell did you get in here?"

"Fell in," chuckled Sleepy. "Can yuh walk?"

"I reckon so."

Sleepy led the way back to the ladder and showed Hashknife where he had fallen in.

"And I never touched the sides," laughed Sleepy. "I'm the champion diver of the world."

"Kinda looks like yuh was," said Hashknife. "Let's get out of here, before they come lookin' for me. Got a gun?"

"Yeah, I've got mine."

"We've got to get more."

Sleepy went up the ladder first. It was no difficult climb, and he sprawled in the brush, while Hashknife came slowly up, holding with his elbows to the narrow rungs. It was a painful proceeding for him, but he managed to get over the top.

For a while they sat together in the brush, gathering their strength.

"I've got one pretty black eye," declared Sleepy, "and my scalp kinda goes flip-flap in one place, but I'll live I reckon. I wish I knowed where Big Medicine and the boys are. I left 'em on a pinnacle, while I investigated."

"How long ago was that?"

"Just before dark. I don't know how long I slept. Mebbe my clothes are out of style by this time."

He took out his gun and worked the action.

"It's all right," he decided. "Now what'll we do?"

He did not ask Hashknife for the details of what happened since he had been knocked down in the K-10 ranch-house. The past could wait to be talked about.

"I didn't get a look at the outside of the place," said Hashknife. "They kept me blindfolded. But they're scared, cowboy. Don't never let anybody tell yuh that Baldy Kern and his crew ain't plumb scared. Torres is there, too, and he's scared. They know damn well that they're up against a hard deal.

"When you got away at the K-10, that ruined it for them. I'll bet yore ears burned a lot of times, over what they said. Baldy thought he had killed yuh. Lee Yung, the Chinaman, is one of their outfit. Faro Lannin' is down there, too. I dunno where he fits in but he's not one of Baldy's outfit. There's another big Mexican called Gonzales. I owe him somethin' for givin' me a drink of hooch. Boy, I shore needed it just then. Well, let's go."

"Is Jack Hill down there?" asked Sleepy.

"Yeah, only his name ain't Hill; it's Meline. His dad is one of the big guns of this smugglin' layout."

Sleepy laughed softly, as they started down through the brush.

"It kinda looks like we had some job ahead of us," he whispered. "But it's a job that has to be done, I reckon."

The trip down the side of that bluff was no easy task, but they finally struck the flat ground at the corner of the shed, and crawled through the corral fence. It was light enough to distinguish the colors of the horses, and Hashknife chuckled at sight of his tall gray.

"I heard 'em talkin' about that gray, Sleepy," he said. "It seems that Baldy tried to ride it and got ditched good and proper."

"I seen him rise and glide," laughed Sleepy. "I was lookin' back at the time. One of 'em was throwin' lead at me, but never come within six feet of hittin' me or the horse."

Cautiously they circled the corner and surveyed the triangular yard. From within came the dull rumble of voices. Hashknife pointed at the opposite end of the L.

"That's the kitchen end down there," he whispered. "Might be a good idea to take a look in there, eh?"

They crossed the yard and drew up close to the end window. The light from the open fireplace illuminated the room fairly well, and a glow of light showed through the doorway which led into the other room.

"Look at that table," whispered Hashknife. "There's a whole raft of guns on it. C'mon."

As they drew back from the window, Lopez came in from the other room and started toward the kitchen door. Hashknife and Sleepy ran to the door, where they flattened against the wall.

Lopez swung the door open, stepped out and reached for the jug, which he had placed just outside, and went sprawling without a sound, when Sleepy's sixshooter barrel swished down across the top of his head.

"One gone to seed," whispered Hashknife, as they crossed the threshold and over to the table, where they helped themselves to the guns which had been taken away from Big Medicine's outfit.

Hashknife shoved one inside the waistband of his overalls and took one in each hand, while Sleepy put one in his holster and one in each hand.

"Dressed to kill," breathed Hashknife. "And we wish them all a happy evenin'."

CHAPTER
SEVENTEEN

LIKE A MAN

Big Medicine sprang to his feet as Guadalupe herded Lucy and Wanna into the room, but Kohler drove him back with a rifle barrel.

"Set down!" growled Baldy. "We gave yuh a front seat, and what more do yuh want? Set down and take yore medicine, you big fool! This ain't United States."

"You'll pay for this, Kern," said Big Medicine.

"Oh, all right," laughed Baldy. "Anyway, you won't be here to see it, so don'tcha worry about me. Get up here, Gonzales, and let's get this thing over."

Gonzales slouched to the front and tried to take Wanna by the arm, but she avoided him.

"Stand still!" snapped Baldy. "Yuh don't want to be tied, do yuh? C'mere, priest."

Father Francisco came forward slowly. He seemed very pale in the yellow lamplight; and his lips were set in a determined line.

"I refuse to perform this ceremony," he said slowly. "It is against the laws of God and man to do this thing."

"Oh, the hell it is!"

Baldy gritted his teeth and grasped the priest by the arm, causing him to wince with pain.

"You go right ahead and perform this marriage ceremony, or there'll be one priest runnin' loose in Mexico without ears."

"You would not dare!"

"Wouldn't I?" Baldy laughed sneeringly. "Why wouldn't I? I'm neither snivelin' Catholic nor bawlin' Protestant. You don't mean anythin' to me, pardner. You do as I say, or suffer the consequences."

Baldy drew out a huge pocketknife, opened a blade, and tested it on his thumb. Father Francisco knew that this man was just drunk enough, heartless enough, unprincipled enough to follow out his threat.

"I will do it under protest," said the priest slowly. "It will be no marriage to be sanctioned by God nor by man; words which may as well be spoken by any of you for all they may mean."

"Thassall right," grinned Baldy. "I reckon we'll have plenty of witnesses to prove that a priest done the job all proper."

Gonzales grasped Wanna by the arm and whirled her around, a laugh on his thick lips, when the lamplight flickered on a twisting blade, and Gonzales staggered back clawing at his thick neck.

Torres had missed again. The guard on the knife had struck Gonzales in the neck, but the point had missed by an inch.

With a roar of rage Gonzales whipped out a revolver. Torres had darted toward the door, but Gonzales's bullet struck him and he went sidewise, slithering along the adobe wall, and fell on his face.

"That was close!" whispered Gonzales hoarsely, feeling of his throat.

The crowd was shocked for a moment. Baldy went to Torres and turned him over, but came back quickly.

"Good shootin'," he said coldly. "That settles the argument, Gonzales, so we'll go ahead."

The priest was so badly shaken that he stared dumbly at the outstretched body of Torres, and his lips moved in prayer. Baldy touched him on the arm and motioned for him to proceed. Gonzales had released Wanna when the knife guard had struck him, but now he grasped her again.

But before the priest could begin the ceremony, Jack Meline stepped out from the wall, his bloody lips twisted strangely, and sent a bullet from a heavy revolver into the body of the big Gonzales.

It was so unlooked for that no one moved. Gonzales turned on his heel, a look of wonder on his cruel face. He did not seem to know what had happened. It seemed as if he were waiting for someone to explain. Then he went to his knees and sprawled sidewise, his huge hands gripping at the dirt floor.

Jack had not moved after the shot. The gun was still tensed at his side, a trickle of smoke coming from the muzzle.

"My God, what did yuh do that for?"

Baldy's voice seemed high-pitched, querulous. Doctor Meline moved ponderously toward Jack, peering at him.

"You fool, have you gone mad?" he demanded. "Do you realize what you have done?"

Jack stepped against the wall, covering the doctor with the gun. "I know what I've done," he said hoarsely. "Don't make me do it again."

"By God, he's gone loco!" exclaimed Baldy.

"I'm not crazy." Jack shook his head.

"Go back," he warned his father. "Go back before I shoot."

Lucy and Wanna drew away, but no one tried to stop them.

"Somebody shoot the damn fool," ordered Baldy.

"He's crazy, I tell yuh."

"What's the matter, Jack" asked his father. "Put down that gun. Why are you acting like this?"

"Go ahead and shoot me, if you want to," said Jack, ignoring the doctor's questions.

"Stuck on the girl yourself, eh?" sneered Horan.

But Jack refused to debate the question. No one made a move to draw a gun. Kohler and Horan both held rifles in their hands, but something told them that this white-faced kid might shoot straight.

"It was a dirty deal," said Jack evenly. "I've been raised to admire dirty deals, but this one was more than I could stand. I never had a chance to live honest. Until lately I've never had any ambition to be anything but a crook.

"I don't know why I've changed. God knows, I've no reason to help Big Medicine, except that he was right and I was wrong. They were good to me as long as I was good. I went away hating all of them. I hated them

210

until I seen you trying to marry that girl off to a dirty Mexican crook, and then something made me hate all of you. I'm no better than you are. I know that. But even if I am, I hate you, and I'll block your dirty game as long as I can stand up."

"Jack, you're crazy!" Meline's voice broke. "Crazy, I tell you."

"I'm not crazy."

"You're full of dope!" declared Baldy.

Jack laughed softly, but shook his head.

"No, I'm not, Kern. I was one of my father's free customers before I got shot. I've had one dose since — no more. God knows why he taught me to use it, but he did."

Doctor Meline shook his head, as if to deny it all, turned away, but whirled suddenly and flung himself at Jack. It was almost a surprise assault, but not quite. Jack pulled the trigger as they clinched, and the big man staggered back gripping his right forearm, where the heavy bullet had smashed its way through.

Big Medicine sprang to his feet, but Kohler was into him rifle upraised, just as Baldy drew and fired at Jack. He was too close to miss. Jack sagged back, throwing a hand up to his face, and the next instant Baldy Kern whirled drunkenly, grasping at the table, while from the connecting doors came the heavy report of a sixshooter.

It was Hashknife and Sleepy coming toward the crowd, shooting through their own smoke, taking the K-10 outfit so by surprise that they were stunned into inaction for a moment.

Kohler went down, almost falling into Big Medicine, who caught Kohler's rifle, and leaned against the wall, shooting from his hip. Ike yelped joyfully and flung himself headlong across the floor to get possession of Baldy's sixshooter, while Musical and Cleve almost fought each other to see which might get a chance to use the gun which was still in Kohler's holster.

The room was choked with smoke, through which darted flicks of flame, and the old adobe walls fairly shook from the concussion of the guns.

Then the reports ceased. It was like the touching off of a pack of firecrackers, a blending of many explosions for several seconds, which died away to individual reports, unevenly spaced — then silence.

Smoke clouds drifted past the oil lamp. A man coughed rackingly; someone breathed heavily like a runner after a long race. Hashknife and Sleepy came into the yellow fog around the table, peering through the haze.

"I think," said Musical hoarsely, breaking the silence, "I think I got the son of a gun that busted my 'Holy City'."

He was on the floor beside the table, but now he got to his feet, peering at Hashknife and Sleepy. Big Medicine joined them. He had a bullet scrape across his cheek and there was blood on his right arm, where the sleeve had been torn away.

"Is everybody through?" queried Ike.

He and Cleve came into the lamplight.

"All through, I reckon." said Hashknife wearily. "I wish this smoke would clear."

212

Ike stumbled over, opened the door, and the air cleared rapidly. The priest had fallen back against the wall but now he came to them, his face ashen.

"It has been a big night, *Padre*," said Musical.

"A night of terror," mumbled the priest. "A terrible thing."

"Could 'a' been worse," smiled Sleepy. "We might 'a' been down there on the floor — with them."

The priest shuddered as Hashknife took the lamp and looked over the finish of the fight. There was little doubt of the outcome. Faro Lanning was still alive, as was Torres. The Pinnacle gambler squinted up at them, a painful grin on his thin lips.

"The hand is played out," he said wearily. "You win. I've always stayed until the last pot was played."

"I'm sorry, Faro," said Big Medicine. "I didn't know you were in on the deal until tonight."

"Not their deal," said Faro. "Torres, Reed, Garcia, and myself were together. Blair was with us, too. He was the one who stole Meline's letter to Baldy Kern, tellin' Baldy about sendin' you a package. It was a take package. We found it out. It said that Meline's son was comin' along, and Baldy was to send the package back by him. It would save any chance of a slip.

"Reed shot young Meline. It was a cold-blooded thing to do, but Reed hated Meline. The holdup netted us nothing. It was the four of us that took the cargo away from Baldy's outfit, and we almost got caught by the revenue officers.

"It was the four of us that planned to send you out after rustlers, while we tried to find the cargo. Olsen is a crook, but he didn't belong to either side. For five dollars he would do almost anything, and keep still. He knew we were goin' to hold up the stage that night. Torres wanted the girl, so we helped him take them away."

Torres had nothing to say. He knew that he was going fast, so they left him to the priest and went to the women. Wanna was crying, but Lucy, still stoical, held out her hand to Big Medicine, and they looked at each other. She did not show the least emotion, except that a faint smile passed her lips.

"Lucy," said Big Medicine slowly, "there are times when I thoroughly appreciate you."

She looked at him and turned her head away slightly.

"Sometimes," she said slowly.

Ike had been doing a little investigating on his own hook, and now he came back. "That damned Guadalupe got away, I reckon," he said. "He ain't among the pile nowhere."

"Let him go," said Hashknife. "Mebbe it's a good thing. He can come back and take care of his friends."

Big Medicine held out his hand to Hashknife.

"I haven't thanked you, Hartley," he said. "You and Stevens showed up at the right moment, and it was your work that made it possible for us to get started."

"Don't thank me," said Hashknife. "Thank Sleepy. He fell into the cave and found me. And yuh might give a little thanks to the feller we called Jack Hill."

"Yes," Big Medicine spoke softly. "He deserves our thanks."

214

"I'd vote that we go home," said Musical. "There's nothin' we can do here. Faro and Torres cashed in their last white chip."

"Yes, we'll go home," said Big Medicine wearily. "Home will seem good after all this. Come, Lucy, Wanna. We're going home again, but we are not going to stay home all the time. We are going to travel more. Wanna, you'll see the cities, wear pretty clothes. I'll have the old ranch-house torn down and a new one built. We'll begin to live now!

"I've got plenty of cattle left. We'll trail a bunch down to Caliente and sell them off. We'll sell some horses, too. As soon as we're able we'll improve the hot springs, and make folks want to come to Hawk Hole. We've been buried for years, but now we're going to dig our way into the sunshine."

He seemed almost incoherent in his promises. Wanna looked at him, her eyes wide with surprise, as he put his arms around her and kissed her on the cheek. It was not at all like him. Lucy grinned and held out her hand to Hashknife.

"*Mahsie*," she said, half-whispering her thanks.

"Yo're shore awful welcome," he said gravely.

"Let's go out the kitchen door," suggested Sleepy, and they filed out into the night.

The stars seemed very close out there in the hills. Somewhere a mockingbird was calling, "*Peter, Peter, Peter, Peter.*"

"Lopez got away, too," said Sleepy.

"That's good," sighed Hashknife. "He was only the cook."

They left Big Medicine with the women and went after the horses. The shed was filled with saddles, and they had no trouble in selecting their horses. The K-10 horses were farther down the trail, so they only saddled for Hashknife, and the two women.

Hashknife led his tall gray out of the corral and around to the yard, where he found Lucy and Wanna together.

"Where's Big Medicine?" he asked.

"He gone back," said Lucy, pointing toward the door.

Hashknife dropped his reins and walked to the doorway. There was only an odor of the powder smoke left. Big Medicine was standing near the opposite wall, looking down at the body of Jack Meline. He did not see Hashknife, so intent was he. Suddenly he reached down, grasped one of the hands, and held it for several moments.

Then he got slowly erect, sighed deeply, and turned to see Hashknife. For several moments they looked at each other. Big Medicine came slowly across the room, stopped beside Hashknife, and looked back.

"What was it, Hawkworth?"

Hashknife spoke in a whisper, realizing that it was something that only concerned Big Medicine.

"The philosophy of ignorance," said Big Medicine slowly.

Hashknife's memory flashed back to the time he had said those same words to Big Medicine.

"You don't mean —"

Hashknife hesitated, looking closely at Big Medicine.

216

"It was twenty years ago," said the big man hoarsely. "Jim Meline was my best friend. I wanted to give the little kid a chance, Hartley. He was too small to remember. I didn't want him to be a half-breed, don't you see?"

"I've saved for him all these years. Meline was investing my money for the boy — I thought. It hurt Lucy."

Big Medicine drew his hand across his forehead, as he turned and looked back at the body, lying in the shadows.

"But she doesn't know, Hartley. She must never know."

Big Medicine choked, as he gripped Hashknife's arm.

"I've got to leave him here, Hartley. Maybe I'll come back some day and find where they put him. But don't you see, I wanted to give him his chance?"

"You did, pardner," said Hashknife softly. "He took his chance when it came along. My God, he went out like a man! What more could you want?"

"Like a man," mumbled Big Medicine. "Like a white man, Hartley."

Big Medicine lifted his head. The boys were coming with the horses, and someone asked for Big Medicine and Hashknife.

"All right, boys," called Big Medicine, "we're coming."

His big hand gripped the sore knuckles of Hashknife, and they went hand in hand back to the horses, which would soon take them out of the land of *manana* and into a better tomorrow for Hawk Hole.

Behind them a mockingbird still called, "*Peter.*" Out at the corral a white-faced priest mumbled a prayer, as he saddled a swayback horse, while within the house the wrinkled face of Guadalupe peered over the edge of the trap door. He looked like a very old monkey, except that few have seen a monkey cry tears. Perhaps they were tears of remorse, but it must be remembered that Torres had promised him one hundred dollars in American gold. *Quien sabe?*